The Prietov file

Jose Luis Laso

translation by
Wim van Zyl

The Prietov file © Jose Luis Laso Fernandez

Cover layout: Ana Laso
Cover pictures from https://unsplash.com/photos/

Edition: Ediciones Laso PW - http://ediciones.laso.pw
Book layout: Jose Luis Laso
Translation: Wim van Zyl

Author details:
http://escritor.joseluislaso.es
email: escritor@joseluislaso.es

ISBN: 9788494920103

Printed On Demand by Amazon

First edition: August 2018

To my beloved son, Angel

INDEX

1. A writer or a story

My first trip to the United States

In September 2014 I embarked on the greatest adventure of my life together with 37 other Spanish people. An 89-day experience that would help me, above all, to find myself, or so I believed at the time.

I was 46 years old and abandoned my whole known world: work, family and friends. I tried to start from scratch with a new venture in my life learning everything about startups and entrepreneurship that New York had to offer.

I have to say looking back that it was very hard because even I did not know what I wanted back then. It also helped that the organization sending us on this trip didn't know either what they hoped to achieve with the trip.

With a serious lack of money and resources to complete the trip I had to rely on the kindness and charity of my travel companions to get by. Determined to make the most of the experience and learn as much as possible, I signed up for all the trips and events on offer that were free of charge or low cost. Such was the trip to Washington DC by bus for a mere 8 dollars. It was not a proper guided tour really, just a round trip by bus. The trick was to buy these tickets well in advance to qualify for discounts and special offers. In addition it was very important to bring your own homemade food along to keep the costs down.

Visit to Washington DC

An icy wind was blowing and I was frozen stiff because of the cold. The day had been very long, starting around 2 O'clock in the morning. I was totally exhausted but very pleased to have seen so many things: the Library of Congress, the Congress itself and parts of the city.

Late that afternoon I found myself alone having lost the rest of my travel companions. The groups were teetering out and getting smaller and smaller. Frustrated that I had been unable to get access to the White House and nervous that I might miss my bus, I made my way back to the bus station. The bus that would take me back to New York and my "strange new family" in Brooklyn.

My fears had been completely unfounded as I arrived well over two hours too early in front of the shopping center that enveloped the bus station.

I had to get rid of the last remnants of the homemade rice I brought along to get into the Capitol. No food is allowed in there. That was a couple of hours ago already and the relief of knowing I was close to the bus stop made me realise that I was really starving.

I wandered aimlessly around looking at the billboards of the food stalls. There were so many possibilities that I had trouble deciding. After a few minutes contemplating which was more important, the price or the size of the dish, I finally decided on a combo dish in a Chinese restaurant containing a fair amount of rice. It came with a soda and was great value for money at just six dollars. The trip was teaching me to be thrifty and really appreciate the value of things.

I took a table in the communal area dotted with small tables and chairs. The small restaurants were in truth like stalls at a market that overlooked a large central area where you could sit down to have your meal. I took out my notebook and pen and placed them to the right of the white polystyrene container with a lid, in which moments before, the cook had put a bed of rice, some vegetables and meat on top.

On the second bite of the not very tasty dish, I noticed two people moving one of the nearby chairs towards my table. They sat down uninvited, occupying the new chair and the extra one that was already at my table. I followed their movements, barely looking up, as it always took me a lot of courage to start a conversation with strangers.

"Forgive me for bothering you, my name is Jeff," the man said to me, using a very polished and colorful American accent. "My girlfriend and I have not eaten in days," he went on, "and we'd like to exchange a fantastic story for a plate of food."

"No surprise there!" I thought but said nothing. It annoys me a lot when people approach me for money. Well... at least this time they were asking for food. How refreshing!

My wife had taught me to be charitable to those in need. I looked at the clock on my cell phone and as there were almost two hours left before the departure of my bus, I looked up and stared at them blankly yet slightly irritated.

His eyes, as green as mine, conveyed a deep sense of peace and tranquility. His unkempt appearance, long beard, thinning hair and scabs did not take away anything from the intensity that infused his eyes, quite the contrary actually.

I looked at his companion. Her run down appearance was not enough to hide the startling beauty of her face. Her eyes were vulnerable like those of a fawn. Her hands were clasping his left arm while his two forearms in turn were resting on the edge of the table that only minutes before had been mine exclusively.

I looked down again after my initial observations and it was then that a deep sense of shame and desolation overcame me. I was very careful and worried about spending the few dollars I had left, but would surely be able to borrow some more money from my relatives just by asking and this couple seemed really desperate…

In an almost reflex act, I left my fork on top of the food and pushed the plate towards them.

"I'm sorry, I'll buy some more later," I mumbled in my thinly disguised Spanish English accent.

Jeff pulled the white polystyrene pack containing the food eagerly towards him. He looked at it as if it were pure gold. I was a little surprised and perturbed that he started eating right away without offering food to her first. At the time I assumed the harsh reality of hunger made us who we really are: animals with very basic needs. I later realised that it was not the case at all.

"Why me?," I ventured to ask when, after a well-heaped spoon, he gave the plate to his companion.

He pointed to my notebook.

"Do you like to write?" He asked.

I nodded and at the same time picked up the notebook and pen from the table. At that moment he made a gesture with his fingers, as if holding a virtual pen, urging me to take notes of what he was about to tell me.

And so he began his story. Right from the start I got caught up in the tale. I now regret not recording it with my cell phone as reference material. I do not really know why I did not. I guess I was a bit overwhelmed in the excitement of the moment.

At times, I had to ask him to repeat over and over again until I understood. I really regretted choosing French over English as a second language at high school. How good it would have been for me now if I were more proficient in English! After these little interruptions from my side, he tried to speak slower and more clearly than before.

At one point he took a break to drink from my soda and eat what his partner had left him. She took over the story where he fell silent eating and pointed to the notebook. At the same time she said: "Take notes, please."

She then started giving me names, addresses and dates in between chewing.

When they had finished eating, he reached into the inner pocket of his shabby jacket and took out folded papers that he set on the table. In an almost reverential ceremony, he began to unfold and smooth them with both hands as if he hoped that the effort would actually return the lost freshness of the paper. When he finished with what looked like a brief farewell he pushed the sheets toward my side of the table like saying "they are for you"

Then I repeated my initial question:

"Why me?"

He explained that they were tired of being on the run and without any resources. They believed that the end of the road was getting closer for them so they could not allow their story to die with them.

When it seemed that our meeting was over, they started to get up and I asked them to wait a moment. I rummaged in my wallet and took out the last twenty-six dollars I still had and handed it to them. At the same time I asked them,

"How can I find you guys?"

"You cannot! They exclaimed in unison. It's too dangerous for you, and for us."

After pausing a moment she continued:

"Handle the matter discreetly, trust no one, and self-publish the story when you have it ready to reach as many people as possible without subjecting it to the censorship of an editor at any stage.

"But I... ," I stammered, "I want to help you guys..."

"You already did, my friend. Publish it, that is all we want."

They got up and left me alone thinking about what they had just told me.

After a while I saw some of my friends from the house in Brooklyn appearing.

"How did it go?" They asked.

Trust no one... her words echoed in my head.

"Well," I said "I got very bored waiting such a long time for you guys to come."

"What are all those papers?" One of them asked me.

With my eyes scanning my surroundings and still struggling to get out of a semi-shock state, I answered mechanically:

"Nothing, just a few notes."

The trip back to New York took almost five hours and I had a hard time digesting what had just happened to me. I was continuously reliving the whole conversation and the mystery surrounding the couple.

Return to New York

After a few days back in Brooklyn I began to work on the manuscript. The truth is that the only thing we had in sufficient quantity in the house, was time. Money and food were in short supply, but time at least, I had in vast quantities. I therefore had no trouble to give shape to that first manuscript.

During our time there I took several trips to Manhattan to research and confirm all the information she gave me. For my roommates, my newfound family in Brooklyn, I used the excuse that I was going to technological meetings. My story was quite credible as it was one of the main reasons for our trip to New York. I even got someone to read the first chapter of the book to see if the story intrigued them. Obviously I led them to believe that it was a completely fictional story with no truth in it whatsoever. I hope that if any of them were to read this years later, they would forgive the white lies I told them.

The initial idea was to have a first draft ready in the months following my return to Spain, but I wanted to take advantage of their life history to really try and establish myself as a novelist. With an already published book about programming and two budding works, I wanted to branch out into an entirely new field for me. I wanted to conjure up a level of drama and intrigue enough to really hook the reader.

As you can imagine that couple could not really give me enough detail to cover the whole embroiled history in the short expanse of just over an hour. They did give me the backbone and outline from where to start. My eagerness to write, the documentation and my subsequent research allowed their experiences to come alive on paper flowing into a natural sequence of events.

In the back of my head I knew full well that I couldn't have been the only unsuspecting tourist with a notebook and pen who gave up a plate of food in exchange for the same story. Actually, I would have done the same in their shoes. For two reasons mainly: to be able to eat and to spread the story as far and wide as possible. As my colleague aptly observed on several occasions later: Why not just choose a journalist? Indeed yes, but I don't think they were actually spoilt for choice at the time. In addition, a journalist would have demanded to keep in contact with them and exclusive rights to the information. I do not really know, maybe I was naive, but it happened like that and I am very glad it did..

I hope the end result will engross and surprise enough to give you food for thought. Naturally some information and names were changed to protect people and avoid lawsuits. I can however confirm that the facts provided by them were sufficiently incriminating to warrant the necessary caution from my side.

Even so, I followed their advice and directly published the work without submitting it to the censorship an editor or publisher. Above all I minimize the retail price sufficiently to ensure this history is available to reach the whole world.

I only hope Jeff, if you ever read this, you will forgive me the small writer's liberties I took in presenting your desperation in the chapters that follow.

And so begins their story...

2. The past

March 1992 in an European country

"Basili Prietov, scientific boss of East Dart, also known by the acronym EADAR, was reported missing one week ago. His wife has been here everyday requesting that we do something to find him. His company is also not cooperating," complained the sergeant to the superintendent of the police prefecture.

The superintendent, sitting in his high-back office chair of black imitation leather, rubbed his white beard, leaned back and said in a serious tone:

"Why did you not tell me this before?"

"It looked like a routine case, Sir," said the young sergeant looking directly into the strict dark eyes of the boss, "but the clues don't seem to lead anywhere."

"Okay, sit down and tell me everything."

"Well, he is a medium-sized man with short grey hair and a bushy beard. His wife brought this picture in," he said while handing it to his boss. "He is fifty-two years old and has worked for East Dart since before meeting his wife fifteen years ago. They also have an eight year old daughter, Olivia."

"And what about the inquiries we've been carrying out so far, Sergeant?" asked the superintendent.

The sergeant reported how they had made inquiries into his personal and professional life. Questioning of family, neighbors and friends did not reveal any leads. He seemed like a regular family man, unlikely to disappear without a trace. Regarding the professional life, the company had refused to answer any questions alleging the confidentiality of his work. Outside of the company, his colleagues would not cooperate for fear of losing their jobs.

"The company refuses to reveal the scope of the research that Mr. Prietov is working on, or rather was working on. And the clues, as I said, lead us to a dead-end," finished the short sargeant.

"All right, here's what we're going to do, Sergeant. Give this matter top priority. Give the appropriate search commands and spread this picture around. If, in twelve hours we have no news, widen the search radius to neighboring countries. And contact his wife right away and bring her in as soon as possible."

"Done, Sir! She came in this morning and said she wouldn't leave before she spoke to you."

"Then show her in immediately."

A few minutes later a woman of medium height, with long black hair, ostensibly dyed, burst into the commissary's office. She was accompanied by a young girl. He escorted them to the chairs opposite his boss, and then hurried out of the office to carry out his orders.

The name written on the boss' table plate read ALEKSEY IVANOV.

The Commissary stared for a moment at the woman's clear eyes in which all the anguish she was going through could be seen. She was dressed in street clothes, probably from a humble but well-educated family, and it was certainly the clothing with which she went to church on Sundays. He turned to look at the little girl's face, no doubt, she looked so much like her parents, whom he had seen in the picture that the sergeant showed him.

"Ma'am," he began, "please accept my most sincere apologies for the delay in your husband's case. We are somewhat stuck with some urgent cases. However, I have given the appropriate orders to handle your husband's case with the highest priority."

"Please believe me I'm so sorry to disturb you, but Basili has not been at home for days now and I'm really worried," said with voice trembling with concern.

"Do you have other information that we don't know?" the Commissary asked her.

"To tell you the truth, yes. Some days before he disappeared we had a very weird conversation, and it left me very worried and quite perturbed."

Some weeks earlier

Family Prietov was finishing dinner and eating dessert, not a huge quantity of food even though it was enough. It could not be said that this family was rich but they had enough to get by.

Immediately after dinner, before clearing the table, Basili Pietrov took his wife's hand and said:

"Olievna, you have to promise me that in the event something happens to me, you and Olivia will continue your lives without looking back and dwelling in the past."

"Why do you say that? You are scaring me!" said in a shaky voice while he was already looking lovingly at their little daughter.

The young Olivia, with her short blond hair and her big brown eyes, was totally unaware of her father's eyes on her. The advantage when you are eight is that you do not have to worry about adult conversations too much. Besides she did not finish her dessert and was focusing her attention there.

Several seconds passed before Basili broke the silence again.

"Look at her, our little daughter is already becoming a little woman. Although she is only eight she acts very mature for her age," said in a serious tone.

Two involuntary and woeful drops ran from his eyes and got trapped in his dense and dark beard.

With his eyes still burning and red from the emotion he turned to his wife and took her hand again.

"Promise me!" he asked urgently now, "Things are getting very hard and nearly impossible at the company now. I don't want you to get obsessed with looking for explanations in the event that something happens to me. It could be very dangerous for you two," said in the sweetest tone he could muster in his emotional state.

"You are asking me an impossible thing, Basili. Besides you are making me more nervous. Tell me the truth, why are you saying all these things"

They were talking for a long time, late into the night. He, tried to convince her with strong arguments, but she did not want to hear any of his explanations, unaware of the real menace her husband tried to warn her about.

Little Olivia will remember that night for the rest of her life. Oblivious at least in part to all that happened, her subconscious, without any doubt, registered every single word that was said that night.

Some days after that

"Mr. Prietov, good morning!" a familiar voice sounds just behind him.

Without looking up from his desk, Basili interjected abruptly:

"Good morning... Boss"

"I hope, for your sake," the boss made a dramatic pause, "and for your family's sake, that the prototype will be ready in two days. Our patron has high hopes for this project and will come at the end of this week to check that everything is okay and that we are still on track"

"I have already explained to you, boss," he started saying while removing his glasses and putting them on the table. He swivelled his chair around, "that things aren't so easy and simple," he finished to say with his boss now right in front of him.

"I don't care, Prietov! I gave my word that we would meet the deadline," he said in a raised voice now totally angry.

Now his face turned a bright red with anger. His eyes, covered by huge thick glasses glared at Prietov. The green of his eyes now contrasting sharply with the red of the veins, showing his intense anger. Although he was much younger than Prietov, his boss' hair was totally white.

During the last days all the conversations between them ended in an argument. Basili already realized that the only path to freedom was to not allow his arm to be twisted. He knew what the consequences would be if he didn't obey, but he was convinced that it will be worse if he did. He would be trapped - a slave for life.

"So... do whatever you have to do but I tell you well in advance that the prototype won't be ready at the expected date," he swiveled back on his chair to focus on the work in front of him on his table.

He was now unable to see the reaction of his boss. His face was totally red with rage, he grimaced and he clasped his hands tightly into fists, sweat forming on his forehead. If he could, he would have throttled the life from Prietov right there and then to get rid of him.

But he needed this *genius*..., at least for the moment. There was no one else in his organization good enough to solve that convoluted gibberish. It was more than probable that even Prietov would not be able to find the solution. He could not shed the thought that Prietov was stalling just to buy himself some time.

He almost felt sorry for the man, because if it were true he was going to regret it dearly.

He turned on his heels and headed for the hall, where a visitor was waiting to talk about other matters. He hoped to calm himself down before meeting him.

Weeks later when the police got a statement from one of Prietrov's colleagues, who refused to talk at first, it became clear that that was one of the pivotal moments that several people remembered as the key to the mystery.

The boss on the other hand did not release any official statement and the company's lawyers were instructed to use any loophole available to them to lay claim to all the possible clauses of confidentiality of sensitive information available to them to prevent any information from becoming public. Until any evidence of a crime could be found, there was absolutely no way of blaming anyone, let alone the company.

Some days later in a neighboring country

Alex had been in the police department for more than ten years. He loved his job. He always felt that he was born to be a policeman. His skills of deduction were only short of superhuman, according to those who knew him well. He graduated from the academy with grades that were totally off the charts. Bearing in mind his age it could well be said that he was the youngest on the team.

When Alex entered the apartment he was not at all surprised by the mess and chaos that met his eyes. The room was totally ransacked and a couple of police officials pored over what he assumed to be the body in the background. He glanced around with a trained eye to get an idea of what he was facing.

A small entrance hall lead off the front door and connected the dining room or main room, he was still undecided about the layout of the flat. He could see a very austere decoration with a small hook just to the right of the door as the door opened to the left. He immediately assumed it was there to hang up the keys when entereing the house. The scratch marks under the hook suggested that it had been designed exactly for that purpose. He was not sure at that precise moment if it had been used recently. It could well be that the flat had been acquired recently and its current owner, even without using it, would not have bothered to take it away. Something strange, he thought.

There are certain habits that are very deeply entrenched. This small detail suggested that the one who placed such a hook near the door came from a large family in which they never left the key inside the lock as it could prevent the entering of the father or a brother. The dim light in the hallway undoubtedly came from the open door to the other room from where the already muted rays of the sun shone through a window. He looked up and could see that the bulb still hanging with two wires from the ceiling appeared to be melted. He gestured to one of his companions and pointed to the bulb.

"We've already checked it and it's melted. The sergeant has said that we are not to touch it while there is still daylight available, and to take care of bringing a portable light as soon as possible," the fellow said.

Apart from the strange hook and the bulb, the hall did not have anything else of interest. It could be that the owner was a very spartan person or simply that he had recently moved in and not got around to decorating the apartment. The inspection of the main room would give some clue on this aspect, or so he hoped.

He crossed the few yards to the dining room door and thrust his head into the room, as if waiting for someone from inside to invite him in. He knew that this was not going to happen, but despite the time he had in the police force he still felt a certain unease when he invaded the privacy of the victims in that way.

From that angle he could establish, almost immediately, that the victim had been dragged to where he was, near the window. He considered various theories for what the motive could be for doing such a thing. The one that seemed the most probable, at first at least, was that there was not enough light where the murder took place.

"The corpse had the fingerprints removed with acid and the face is totally disfigured. It will be very difficult to identify the body," said a fellow police official as he approached the body.

Despite all his efforts and that of his colleagues, the case eventually landed in the "UNSOLVED CASES" basket on the boss's desk.

Almost two months later, scanning through all the incoming faxes, Alex noticed the report and photo of a missing person that the prefecture of the neighboring country had sent through a few weeks ago.

Alex moved heaven and earth to find the whereabouts of the corpse found a couple of months ago. As the case was still unsolved, he wanted to have it located to start the appropriate negotiations.

"Hello?.... Yes, referring to the missing person fax sent by your prefecture exactly 23 days ago... I think we have found Mr. Prietov," said Alex to the spokesperson from the neighboring country, "Well, no problem, you can send anyone you want."

The next day a woman arrived at the police station and asked for him.

"Good morning, ma'am. I regret making you come all this way under these circumstances. I hope it is not your husband, although by the description we received and the way in which he died I am afraid that it might be related. Follow me," Alex felt deep sympathy for the woman.

Alex, although very young, has unfortunately on more than one occasion been the bird of ill omen that had to communicate the bad news to a grieving family. As he passed the door of the office he could see a girl of about eight or ten years old raise her head when Mrs. Prietov passed by and she gestured.

"Who is she?" asked Alex

"It's my daughter, Olivia."

"What? Have you really brought your daughter along to come and identify your husband's body?" he said perturbed as he turned to her and showing his harder, more official side.

"You know, I have no one to leave her with, and after what happened, I really don't want to leave her alone at home." Mrs Prietov looked vulnerable and somewhat frightened.

Alex frowned and shrugged as he turned and walked back through the door again.

"I'm Alex," he introduced himself, "Your mother is going with me to take care of some business. Come with me, please, I don't want anything to happen to you. You're going to stay with a friend of mine while we are gone."

And he accompanied the girl to his colleague's office.

"Please, take care of Olivia, I'll be back in a matter of minutes"

Olivia's mother saw from the entrance hall what had just happened.

"Thank you so much, truly, you are very kind"

"You're welcome. I apologize for my previous rudeness. I should not have been so hard on you. I can't imagine what the two of you must be going through."

When entering the cold enclave of the morgue an official pulled out a drawer of one of the stainless steel body fridges marked with a big X and a date.

Olievna slowly moved closer to the drawer and began to cry immediately. She took her husband's hand and knelt beside his body weeping uncontrollably.

"It's him," she said finally when the tears allowed her to utter a few words.

Alex signaled to the official, who left the drawer open and

withdrew a respectful few yards.

"Ma'am, there's no hurry. Take the time you need," and he also took a few steps away.

After a few minutes the woman looked at the policeman with tears cascading like waterfalls and told him that she was done and that they could close the drawer up again.

"Don't worry, we'll start the proceedings immediately so you can bury your husband properly."

Later, in the office, and more composed she dared to ask.

"Tell me, good man. How did he die?"

"We think he was suffocated, though the evidence was inconclusive to really determine the cause of death. It could also have been poisoning, the result would have been the same. His fingerprints were removed with acid. They were quite determined that nobody would be able to identify him."

On the way to the adjoining office, Alex took Olivia's hand and told her.

"Honey, you must be strong and help your Mom. She now needs you more than ever."

The image of the man's bright eyes was forever etched in the girl's eyes and mind.

3. The client

New York, 2012

[6:51pm]

He had trouble sleeping for the past two days. The stress was getting the better of him and he was never at his best if he did not get at least seven hours of sleep per night. Client's web launch was looming and he was stuck. The error in the code was taunting him and the solution remained elusive.

Sitting in front of his terminal the minutes passed. He thought about recent events and how things have gone this far. He had to get down to work, but he was overcome by a feeling of total inertia and frustration.

He gazed mesmerized at the clock in the hallway as the seconds ticked by. He found himself in a state of semi-hypnosis induced by the mechanic device on the wall and drifted off into deep thought. Images from the past flashed through his mind as if it were a slideshow. An image of Rose appeared as she looked that day on Coney Island. The sun was shining warmly on her face and her big brown eyes were shielded by disproportionate large sunglasses. Her delicate skin had already acquired some rosy color, so it must have been mid-summer. The intense green of the bikini enhanced the incipient tan of her skin.

Without even realizing it, the end of the working day arrived and Jeff, totally engrossed in his thoughts, did not notice the grim figure of a man hovering behind him. He was peering over Jeff's shoulder at his screen as if staring intensely enough would explain exactly what the code segment Jeff was working on entailed. What the man did not realize was that Jeff was not at all thinking about the code. He was very far away on Coney Island with his beloved Rose.

The man was wearing a 1950s style charcoal felt fedora, paired with a long lead grey raincoat. To complete the picture he was carrying a black umbrella in his right hand that gave him a fashion magazine appearance. It was quite rare these days to find people who appreciate fashion let alone dressed accordingly. The scene looked like something from the 1920s.

Jeff was oblivious of his surroundings, totally absorbed in his thoughts, staring expressionless at his terminal. The voice of Linda, the security officer on duty, abruptly awoke him from his dream world. She was giving instructions to the overdressed man standing behind Jeff. She assumed that the haughty gentleman had some connection with Jeff, given the proximity to his table and the attention he was paying to what was going on on his computer screen. She did not suspect anything untoward, but nevertheless looked into Jeff's eyes signalling that he had to get rid of his unknown visitor. For an instant, Jeff noticed Linda's eyes, a deep green, unlike Rose's big brown eyes he was looking into seconds ago on the beach in a wonderful daydream of happier times. He tried to imagine Linda being Rose but it didn't quite work. He has missed Rose ever since he broke up with her. Linda had been coming on to him regularly. Women in New York are quite emancipated and not prim at all .

"Our offices will be closing in a few moments, Sir," Jeff heard.

Startled, he turned his head to meet the gazing cold eyes of the imposing stranger behind him. It was a grey so translucently clear that he involuntary thought the man to be an albino. The stranger did not appear apologetic or perturbed in any way at all. There was nothing in his expression that indicated any emotion whatsoever.

Something in those cold eyes reminded him of someone, but he was so focused on his own problems at that moment that he was unable to make any logical connection. The man looked directly at Jeff for a couple of seconds. There was no hint of any guilt in his eyes, no surprise, nothing at all. On the contrary, it rather appeared as if the unannounced visitor was simply doing a routine job that had been rudely interrupted by the security officer. He nonchalantly started walking away, passing a few inches from Jeff's desk.

Jeff watched intrigued as the stranger walked away to the hallway and the lift lobby beyond that. The rhythmic but soft clatter of the disappearing footsteps fixed his gaze and attention until he finally lost sight of the man. At first glance he did not seem tall at all. First impressions can however be very deceiving and he had no clear idea of the stature and height of the visitor until he passed underneath the central arch of the corridor. He was a slender and rather tall man. Hours later they would concur on the description of the sinister gentleman. When the figure finally disappeared completely from his view and the footsteps fell silent, he noticed that Linda was touching his shoulder to attract his attention.

"I'm going to complete my rounds," she said, "Let's talk later." She looked at him quizzically for a moment as if waiting for him to say something.

If ever there were a moment to say something, that was it. But he was so engrossed in what had just happened that he did not really notice the girl with the perfect figure and long brown hair. Today she was wearing it all tied back as she almost always did at work, but he knew full well that beneath that stern hairstyle was a huge, wavy mane. It was true that they could have made a near perfect pair, but it was not exactly the best time to think about new love affairs. It felt as if his relationship with Rose ended so recently, but in truth it was already going on one year.

His mind drifted away again. Linda's bright green eyes lingered in his thoughts and long forgotten memories suddenly resurfaced. He vividly recalled his aptitude tests for admission to the agency. Two people were conducting the tests. A man and a woman formally dressed in dark business suits which were the standard attire of the agency made him perspire through every pore of his skin: *We are believers.*

He survived the spine chilling interview, but could never forget the icy eyes devoid of any emotion of one of his examiners. The immense pressure he was under had no doubt left a lifelong scar on him. Even though he knew his grades were amongst the best in the academy, a real-time test like that was much worse than he'd ever imagined. Nerves almost got the better of him and he came very close to giving up altogether. The man's eyes portrayed a mixture of cruelty and tranquility. The very same thing he saw earlier in the eyes of the stranger beside his table, scrutinizing his work.

It was at times like that when Jeff most hated his company. It was not entirely clear whether placing his desk in the middle of a corridor was due to a lack of resources, as he had been led to believe, or intended as a kind of warped punishment for past behavior. He knew that there were a few more cases like his, both in New York and Illinois, but he found it rather hard to believe that a company that made hundreds of thousands of dollars a day would let it's employees work at tables in a corridor.

The real problem was that the bosses approved this arrangement. He had often spoken about it with Daniel, his direct superior, and Mr. Walker, the Office Manager but they completely disagreed with him, suggesting that they could do nothing. In any case, it had been such a long time in such contra-productive conditions that it ceased to matter to him. The absurdity of it all faded into the background and didn't bother him as much as it initially did. He still remembered when they asked him if they could use his office for a few weeks. He willingly agreed. He had been working for the company for two years at the time and believed in a kind of live and let live attitude. But then he saw that his office began to fill up with more and more people. It was totally ridiculous how, in the space that he himself occupied previously, up to four people now worked.

What was abundantly clear to him though was that this strange incident would not have occurred if he had arranged a table for himself in one of the offices. Although, to be honest, he should have been more careful and alert. It is not normal for someone to stand next to you, a few inches from your table and you don't notice it at all.

Time passed quickly mulling about the events of the day . Time that he really did not have. His boss was hoping that he would be able to fix the bug in time to push it into production before midnight on that stressful Wednesday. Wednesdays were usually a cause for celebration for him as it signalled the halfway mark of the week. It seemed that getting to Wednesday was tough as time dragged on forever, but once there, the rest of the week flew by. But definitely not this one. Things had been twisted in an eerie way.

Going back to the truth.

[8:00pm]
Anticipating possible complications and delays he warned his roommate well in advance not to worry if he did not come home. It was certainly not the first time he would spend the night at the office because of work.

He already spent way too much time reviewing the same segment of code over and over again. He was fatigued and couldn't think straight anymore. He thought it best to stretch his legs and get a soda from the vending machine. He hoped to get a new perspective and that the solution will come to him, as had happened on so many other occasions in the past. It often lead to heated arguments with his friends and colleagues insisting that his work required a certain amount of intuition. It was clear that his perfection of this technique and in-depth knowledge of patterns allowed him to solve the algorithms that he faced in a systematic way. But on a few occasions, certain problems had an elusive solution that even the application of the try and error technique could not solve. Or as it often happened to him, he eventually arrived at a concise and readable solution when some days have passed after implementing some piece of code.

It was a difficult argument open for much contention. Similar to the eternal debate whether animals have intelligence or not. But he was convinced that intuition was required in his line of work. Moreover, interspersed bouts of inspiration had allowed him to solve things in an elegant and sometimes extremely creative way, so much so that he even received an award for his work.

Those were the thoughts Jeff had going through his head on the way to the vending machine. He could not get the image of the austere stranger standing at his desk from his mind. Those eyes reminded him of someone, he was sure of that.

Standing in front of the vending machine and about to insert the coin, his thoughts wandered away from there again... January in Bryant Park, skating together. The cool air penetrated his earmuffs as he tried to disguise the effect of the low temperature by doing some silly pirouette. He still could not understand why he hasn't left this cold place for warmer climes. Undoubtedly a land of opportunities like the United States should allow him to relocate without any problems to another more sunny spot in the country. Of course Rose would not be able to accompany him... Hand in hand, she asked him to buy her a hot chocolate to warm her up to which he lovingly agreed. With a gaunt gait, like all those who came off the skating rink with their skates on, he went to the rest area. Waiting his turn at the vending machine he lost track of time thinking about all the time they have been together. Surely it was high time to tell her how he felt about her and that he wanted her in his life permanently.

The buzzing of the machine, indicating that he had to make his choice, brought him back to reality from his memories of Rose. He inserted the code for a soda and waited for the can to fall rumbling into the collection bay. He retrieved it absently from the machine and took a small sip. He returned to his table and poured the contents into his cup. He preferred to drink soda from it rather than from the cold can. Complicated yet methodical, he sometimes wished he was not all that predictable. Sticking to all his old habits made him feel that they were somehow still together.

He switched on the screen of his terminal again and took a long sip from the cup. As he was typing in the characters making up his password, his vision suddenly became blurred and he blacked out as his head dropped to the table.

[10:30pm]
"He's asleep. The drug has taken the desired effect. I was not entirely sure that he would use the cup though. It seems that intelligence did its job well. Old habits die hard they say and it played right into our hands"

"Yes, we must act with caution. Look at which line the cursor stopped by, and photograph as much as you can."

"We have to copy all the contents of the hard drive as well as this external hard drive. It has a device connected to it that looks like a charger."

"Take note of the exact position of everything and ensure that we leave it exactly the way we found it."

"I'm not a rookie. What do you take me for?"

"This idiot!" He grumbled. I don't know why I always have to put up with bumbling newbies. And to top it all he thinks he knows everything already. I hope he doesn't ruin it like the previous one, because I won't take the blame again.

The other ignored the mumblings of his colleague, and went on with what he was doing.

[7:30am]
Jeff lifted his face from the table with an unusual heaviness. His eyes were cloudy and he felt dizzy. He put his head back on the same spot, still warm. He had a severe headache, worthy of a great hangover. The last thing he remembered was that he took a sip of his soda, but the rest was still in the cup. The drink was however not cold anymore.

He checked, with great difficulty, the space on top of his desk. He was looking for something strange, something out of place that might catch his eye. But everything was as he left it. He had a hard time trying to remember what happened and felt woozy and numb. He could not keep his eyes open and shut them at intervals. He looked at the clock in the hallway and could not believe the time. Surely it had only been a few minutes since he dropped his head to have a light rest. There was no sign of anything out of place.

He leaned back in the chair trying to compose himself. He felt like a train wreck. He could not control his movements yet, so he decided to wait for his body to catch up before attempting to stand. He knew he did not sleep properly for many days but never before has he fallen asleep at his desk and certainly not for hours on end. It was the first time something like this happened to him.

[8:00am]
The first employees began to arrive in dribs and drabs for the working day entering through the front door and and traipsing

into the hallway where his table was located. At that moment he really became aware of the time. The offices opened at 8 in the morning. Still drowsy, he tried to stand up in a very awkward fashion. He straightened his crumpled shirt a little and ruffled his hair. With a carefree gesture he went to the toilet to wash his face and fresh himself up a little.

What he saw in the mirror left him speechless: his face, still creased by the cracks in the table against which he had slept, showed obvious signs of having ingested some allergenic substance. Jeff had a rare condition. It practically produced a violent allergic reaction to most substances. In fact, the soda he ingested last night was nothing other than an isotonic drink.

The symptoms were obvious: swelling and redness on various parts of the face, inflammation of the eyelids and jaundiced eyes. His tongue seemed swollen and stiff.

In a moment of lucidity, he fished out his cell phone from his pocket and took a few photos. He stared at his own reflection in the mirror for a moment. He was really curious as to why it so much resembled the time he was drugged in Warsaw. Ever since his training this had always seemed to be a suicide mission. He blinked to come out of his reverie.

He returned to his table with his face washed but with obvious signs of weariness. His head still ached with a continuous feeling of hammering and pounding. He reviewed his situation. He picked up a piece of paper to write down everything he remembered from the night before, including the strange visitor who seemed to have had an unusual interest in what he did.

He wrote placing the paper directly on the table, so as not to leave prints of his writing on another piece of paper. He did not really think about it. His previous work experience made him to do these things automatically without even thinking about it. He tried not to press too hard on the pen while scribbling some strange signs. At University he developed his own writing system that allowed him to take notes quickly and thought it was a good time to capitalize on this special skill.

He was still contemplating whether the lack of sleep could have induced hallucinations and caused him to collapse at his desk from total exhaustion. There were the signs of intoxication though and some or other allergic reaction to consider. Then again the reaction could have been aggravated by age. Could it be possible that even the isotonic drink will affect him now?

He was about to abandon when he noticed the flashing cursor on the screen of his terminal. For a moment he was stunned and a little perplexed by the constant rhythm of the cursor in the upper left corner of the screen, next to the word "Login:" He felt himself strangely drawn to it - almost mesmerized. The monotony of the flickering brought him back to reality and the present moment, putting aside all that had happened.

The cursor beckoned him to enter his username and password to access the system, which he automatically did as he had done hundreds of times before, that same week. The security system of the company required a forced log-off from all users to block the screens before leaving their tables.

The monitor blinked briefly to present the work session as it was when it locked the screen last time. The VIM editing pointer was still on the same line of code that he remembered before he passed out, probably from exhaustion.

[8:30am]
He looked at the clock in disbelief. How could it be? More than twelve hours have passed since he blacked out at his desk and woke up totally disoriented. In those twelve hours the cursor in the text file where he was trying to fix the complex and elusive error did not move forward or backward.

"Damn!" he said to himself. He relived the situation in his head and then scribbled what appeared to be a list onto the paper. He was jotting down the names of people he recalled being on duty the previous night. And at last, pointing to one of the names, he murmured softly, "Rose".

He got up quietly, but not before locking the screen again and headed down the hall to the reception area, where several young ladies worked. It was a rather large area, like an agora, where two big tables, symmetrically placed, seated two groups of women. As he walked he counted his steps in an obsessive way. It was as if keeping track of his footsteps gave him some peace, having his mind on something else. "Eighty-two" he said to himself. When he reached the table he leaned over the counter and said in a whisper:

"Rose, I need to talk to you right now".

[9:02am]
"Give me a moment Jeff, the chief supervisor requested this report urgently and I need to get it to him within the next half an hour," Rose said in a truly distressed tone.

"All right, I'll wait for you at my table in half an hour. Please hurry up!" He said in a tone raw with despair and anguish.

It was the first time he heard his own voice since he woke up this morning and it gave the impression that he was truly in a sorry state. He returned to his table and tried to open the drawers. They were locked just as he remembered them. He paused for a moment. He did not quite understand the reason why someone, inside or outside of the company, would try to get him out of the way.

He was simply an unimportant developer tasked with the routine reviewing of a bug in a program for one of the company's customers.

"Hold on, that was it! Who was the client?" He said to himself as he tried to remember. He was very bad at remembering these long names that the brand new companies register nowadays. Once the short names were registered, the businessmen used the full name of their idea, without acronyms or anything.

He searched and rummaged through the papers in his file. He

could not find his superior's initial order sheet. He would have to log into the system on his terminal again, but it was very hard to touch what could quite possibly hold important information to explain what happened to him. He did not know who could be involved and whether leaving things intact could help him in the long run or not. He went into a kind of mental loop trying to see how he could resolve the issue.

The sound of his desk phone shook him out of his reverie. Mechanically he hurriedly picked up the receiver and said in a distracted voice:

"This is Jeff."

"Jeff, Daniel here, I have received a call from EUROPE-ASIAN DWELLING ARTIST REUNITED (EADAR) saying that their platform still has the same bug. I thought you stayed last night to fix it..."

That was it and what a name! No wonder I had trouble remembering it, he thought. *And now I have to lie to my supervisor as I'm not willing to be taken as crazy or even worse, as lazy.*

"Daniel, I'm so sorry, something has happened. My computer fried and I've been chasing down the maintenance people all night. Now that the fellows are working, I'm going to ask them to lend me another terminal and I'll finish it quickly. I'll call you as soon as I have one" he said in a tone that did not seem convincing at all.

"Okay, you better do it urgently as I am going to tell the client that they will have it sorted within the hour," Daniel said authoritatively.

After putting down the phone he stared transfixed at the ceiling. He had to solve the program error and fast. But it was more urgent to find out what happened to him and why. The error would surely not take him more than half an hour or so to fix. At last he stopped staring at the ceiling and sat up slightly in the chair.

Jeff pulled out his laptop from it's bag. He placed it on the table after moving the keyboard from his work computer out of the way.

Immediately he set out to google the name of the company. He clicked on the images option of the menu and was scrolling down until one face caught his attention: those eyes...

There was no record of who he might be, but the relationship with the client seemed obvious. He was the very same person who stood for who knows how long next to his desk. He minimized the browser to leave the desktop free, started the terminal application and logged onto the server to see the file that he already knew was still open and with the cursor in the exact position where he left it last night.

If he didn't have his personal computer with him he would have had no other choice but to use the work one. But in this case he preferred to save that ace for when it was really necessary. Now, much more lucid, he was able to discern clearly and see the error. It is incredible what a difference a few hours of rest can make to an analytical mind.

He commented out a couple of lines of code and fixed two others. Finally he saved the changes by pressing the usual keys ':wq' and restarted the *nginx* service and accessed the client's platform to see if the issue was resolved. After a series of mouse clicks here and there and filling in a few text fields, he managed to access the conflict zone and passed the test the first time.

Under normal circumstances or rather, in his previous team, they would never have allowed him to directly edit files in production and much less to approve a test of his own work. The whole application would have been checked from top to bottom by an independent party before approval. Things were much different now since he left his previous team and they were hurrying him along. Besides, something very strange was happening around him lately.

So, when he passed the test, he picked up the phone and dialed internal extension 1012 to speak to his supervisor:

"Daniel, it's Jeff. Issue fixed. Check it when you can and ping the client. And... please, forgive the delay"

"Okay, thank you Jeff. If you don't hear from me assume that everything went well."

Jeff hung up the receiver and looked pensively at the screen of his laptop.

4. Dead end

They had gone, like so many times before, to his flat to watch television for a while. He knew beforehand how these evenings usually ended. It bothered him that they were only intimate when Rose thought it appropriate and that turned out to be very sporadic at best. After their customary cup of tea and checking the television for anything new or interesting, he tenderly put his hand on her leg hoping that she would take it as she has done so many times before. It troubled him a little when this did not happen. Not really knowing what to do next he started massaging her leg gently. He was unsure whether Rose could actually feel his soft touch and the warmth of his hands through her tight jeans.

He pulled her closer to him and gave her a long kiss. He was not sure that he was on the right track but he seemed to be doing well as she was quite responsive to his touch and kiss. The kiss lasted for several minutes increasing in intensity and unleashing a wave of sexual desire in him. After a while she pushed him away gently and spoke. He was jolted from his sensual daydream into the present by her voice:

"Hi Jeff."

Almost thirty-five minutes had passed since he saw her at her desk. She shook him a little to get his attention.

"What was so important?"

The sensual daydream still had a firm hold on his body and mind. He barely avoided the appearance of being caught red handed when he looked up at her. He took a deep breath to compose himself and said:

"Not here. Can you take half an hour to have coffee with me at the bar across the street?"

"Sure, let me notify my colleague with a text message as we go."

Jeff left the table as it had been before: he put his laptop back in it's bag, closed the drawers, and escorted Rose out of the building. On the way, he spoke in a stage whisper about what had happened to him, putting his hand in front of his mouth to obscure the words but without being too conspicuous. The people who knew them were well aware of the fact that they had been together for a while and would make nothing of it.

They crossed the street and when they arrived at the bar she looked at him, her concern very clear:

"I can't believe what you're telling me. How could this have happened? Are you sure, Jeff?"

"That's the problem, I'm not sure myself. I have reason to belief that something happened at my desk last night."

"It makes sense: the drug in the drink, the fact that you don't remember anything, the cursor..."

"Yes," he interrupted, "and don't forget the strange fellow scrutinizing my desk over my shoulder," he went on. "Do you know Linda? The security officer who was on duty yesterday closing the offices?"

"Yes, nice girl," Rose said.

"I have to talk to her and find out whether she remembers anything about that austere character."

After a long coffee and rehashing the strange events Jeff experienced the previous night, they said goodbye at the door of the bar as to raise no more suspicion than was necessary. That afternoon, after leaving work, they met at Rose's house to continue talking about what could be done independently to get to the bottom of the strange incidents without drawing too much attention to their inquiries. Jeff asked her to be careful, keeping things under wraps whilst being on the lookout for anything out of the ordinary.

[10:15 am]
Upon reaching his floor Jeff tried to locate Linda, but she changed her shift and would not arrive until 3pm. He decided to start his investigation pursuing other avenues.

For the first time since he woke up this morning at his table, his mind was truly lucid and unoccupied. As he was unable to talk to Linda and certainly couldn't start his daily chores without shedding some light on his problems, he decided to take the bull by the horns.

The first step would be to open the computer terminal, exit the VIM and see if they had left any trace. If they were as thorough as he suspected, they might not have anticipated that he would be suspicious and start investigating. He promptly proceeded to enter his password and was faced by the cursed cursor blinking in the same row and column as hours ago.

He wrote down the position of the cursor in case it was relevant, left the text editor and launched the history command to get a list of the latest executions requested by the console.

```
490 vim /projects/clients/eadar/app/core.rb
491 ssh 159.81.122.217
492 gem install bgk5
493 service bgk5 start
494 vim /projects/clients/eadar/app/core.rb
495 history
jeff: ~ [2014-11-17 10:30:09]
```

To his amazement he saw that they closed the file he was editing, they connected to a remote server and installed a program, bgk5, on his computer. And to top it all they did not even bother to cover their tracks! That was the very first thing they taught Jeff at the agency. He fished out his cell phone from his pocket and took a couple of photos of the terminal as evidence.

Then he took out his laptop from it's bag and launched a search of the IP address to see if he could obtain more data like domains hosted, country of origin or any other information that could give him an indication of where to look next.

All too soon it became very clear that the IP could not be found. He tried a few more sites but got the exact same result.

```
-> ping 159.81.122.217
PING 159.81.122.217 (159.81.122.217): 56 data bytes
Request timeout for icmp_seq 0
Request timeout for icmp_seq 1
Request timeout for icmp_seq 2
Request timeout for icmp_seq 3
Request timeout for icmp_seq 4
Request timeout for icmp_seq 5
Request timeout for icmp_seq 6
```

Desperate now, he was forced to use his last resort in an attempt to get more information. He knew full well that this was the make or break point and that there would be no turning back after this. Slowly and with rhythmic determination he started typing:

```
ssh 159.81.122.217
```

He deliberately allowed a few milliseconds to pass between the pressing of each key in an attempt to drag out the typing time and to enable him to make a quick retreat at any moment if needed.

Once all the necessary characters reflected on the screen, he hesitantly placed his index finger on the *enter* key. He arched his finger like a trigger and took a deep breath.

He closed his eyes and felt a cool salty breeze caressing his face. He remembered again how, as if it were yesterday on Coney Island, Rose told him that they should take things slower. He opened his eyes, let out a deep breath and then pressed the *enter* key.

The terminal responded with the following message:

ssh jeffpatterson@159.81.122.217's password: _

At this point Jeff held his head rubbing his forehead repeatedly as if this manual action would actually clear his mind and help him to focus.

Normally a system supports three failed password attempts. After that, the security system usually locks you out to prevent attacks from hackers.

He pondered for a long time as to what the password might be. So much so that when he eventually decided to type in a password, the session had expired and he had to start the command again.

This time he knew what he wanted to try. He knew that no one in his right mind would use the universal password to protect a commercial server.

1234

The console took a moment to show the new message:

Last login: Fri Nov 14 22:50:12 2014 from ***
CentOS release 6.4 (Final)

```
Linux oo326471.***.com 2.6.32-358.14.1.el6
server : oo326471
hostname : oo326471.***.com
eth0 IPv4 : 159.81.122.217
```

He was completely stunned. He could not believe that someone was so stupid as to use that password.

But the next thing he saw really blew his mind:

```
Welcome, Jeff Patterson
>/home/jeffpatterson
```

It was totally unbelievable. Apart from the fact that the system welcomed him, he had a profile on that system with his name.

There were two possibilities. Either he had an account on that server, or someone was playing the fool with him.

He immediately closed the session with the Ctrl-D shortcut and was engrossed in deep thought whilst rolling his pen between the thumb and index finger of his left hand. This was undoubtedly a habit that relaxed him. It also allowed him to concentrate on not throwing the pen and prevent it from dropping.

After thinking in circles for some time, he stopped rolling the pen when he noticed something against the ceiling. Near the opposite corner from where he was sitting there was a surveillance camera. He could not believe that he had been so clueless. He could simply have resorted to the security recording to confirm his suspicions.

He jumped up and made his way to the security room. He was not sure how he could ask for this kind of information without raising suspicion, but he pushed himself to continue with the only plan he had at the time.

He knocked on the door of the surveillance office and when he saw Charles coming to the door, his heart almost stopped. He could not believe that out of the almost 300 people who worked in this office of the company he was to run into the only one that he despised. After all these years he had not been able to forget that horrible incident at one of the company parties. Jeff was sure that Charles had not forgotten either. It could be said that he has hated him in silence ever since. Besides, the feeling was mutual.

"Ah, it's you," Jeff stammered, "I'll be back when there's someone else on duty, excuse me."

"I have seen...," Charles began.

"What?"

"You know what I'm talking about, come in".

As soon as he crossed the doorstep he realized he had screwed up. He made a serious blunder to let his archenemy know what he was talking about, and he could not afford such a slip. Now it was too late.

"Sit down," he said, "I know we do not get along, and that... but she really likes me and I know how you two ended up."

"What? Are you talking about Rose...?"

"Yeah right. When I told you that I had seen..., I meant her. She came to me a while ago to ask for a tape of last night's surveillance footage and I told her how I felt about her..."

"What?... A tape?" he stuttered with the confusion clear in his voice.

"Come on, we'll talk about the tape in due course. Rose... okay? I like her and I'm going to ask her out. I hope you don't mind..."

"Oh, yes... don't worry, we've been over for a while... we're just good friends now," Jeff managed to say.

After a couple of minutes they closed the subject of Rose. Charles told Jeff that he gave the tape to her. She told him that it was something that could incriminate a friend.

"She promised to bring it back to me before the change of the shift, otherwise I will be in serious trouble."

When Jeff left the surveillance room, he had almost no pulse. What was going on there?

Almost as if on autopilot he walked to the central hall and felt numbed when he saw that Rose was not at her desk. He peeped over her desk to see whether her purse and coat were hanging on the back of the chair and when he saw no sign of them, he walked over to one of her colleagues.

"Have you seen Rose?"

"She left in a hurry, an important call... I think."

This has never happened before. Not only did she take the lead but also neatly got rid of him. He made his way back to the corridor where his table was.

5. First evidence

[11:57am]
"Jeff," someone shouted from the hallway, "the big boss wants to see you."

"What now?" He said to himself.

He hurried down the hall to take the elevator. When the doors opened he pressed the button for the 42nd floor. As he whizzed upwards, his mind disconnected from reality. He started thinking about how many times he had been in this lift before. He had been in this company for 8 years, working from Monday to Saturday and even some Sundays... That made more than...

DING. The elevator bell shook him back to reality. He left the cubicle and headed for his superior's office.

The austere interior decoration of the company had always been a thorn in his flesh, but the corridor leading to the Head of the New York delegation took it to new heights.

The black and white prints on both sides of the corridor were spaced exactly three metres apart and contained unnerving images. It reminded him of the Rorschach tests used by psychiatrists to determine whether a patient belonged in a straight jacket or not.

In general the designs resembled finger paintings in black ink one would expect to find in a kindergarten where toddlers were allowed to let their creative juices run wild.

Pictures also came to mind of a devious Nursery Director fooling unsuspecting parents with the idea of how creativity aided early childhood development.

And surely the profits of the sale of said works of art went straight into the director's pockets.

He recalled yet another theory he dreamed up the previous time he took this scenic route to the boss' office. That time around he imagined that the eerie paintings actually belonged to an eccentric aristocrat who lost his mansion to settle gambling debts. As the General Director at the time maintained close relationships with the nobility, the horrid paintings were given on loan to the company. Jeff's imagination was spiralling out of control and he had to caution himself back to reality from time to time. Sometimes he regretted his career choice and felt that he would have been much happier as a private investigator or detective.

Still engrossed in his fantasies he found himself suddenly at the end of the corridor.

He hesitated for a moment. Then he knocked softly on the door, and when he received no invitation to enter, he opened the door with great care. In the first office, normally occupied by the secretary, there was nobody. He looked to the left, towards the chief's door and saw that it was slightly ajar.

As the door was not closed, he took the liberty of peeping around the half open door without knocking. He had enough time to jolt back, take a deep breath and knock this time around.

"He's going to see me here...," said a voice almost imperceptibly, but he recognized it straight away.

"It's okay," the chief said aloud, "Come in," he added.

With a careless nod, intended as a greeting, Jeff passed by Rose.

"Did you call me?"

"Yes, sit down."

[12:01am]

His boss briefed him on the subject informing him that the client had called about an incident that occurred in their finance software, which is assigned to the Illinois delegation. He could not understand what an accounting or payroll program had to do with a web platform. He tried to speak to get clarity, but the chief cut him off and continued talking.

"We've been told that they've been attacked by the accounting program from the IP of the platform you're developing." The boss paused for a drink of water, and Jeff could not contain a small shudder.

He went on:

"Although there weren't numerous attacks on the system, the figures involved were staggering...," he returned to wait for a reaction from Jeff, who made a face of total amazement.

"In every attack a million have been transferred," he added, "and there have been thirteen since last night at 11:30 pm. Fortunately, the client has not yet found out."

Jeff, clasped his head in his hands and leaned forward with his elbows on his knees. He felt nauseous. It finally all made sense to him. It was all about money.

He tried to focus. He attempted to think of something pleasant, as he had been taught at the agency. His thoughts immediately wandered off to a sun-drenched beach with clear, crystalline water and a gentle swell. He took three deep breaths and looked up. He looked at his boss and then at Rose, fixed his gaze on her for a moment... until she broke the silence:

"I told him, Jeff. It was too important."

"But... even if I was going to do such a thing, I would still want to know what had happened before I started to create all this confusion...," he replied.

"We've seen the recording, Jeff... there's nothing between 9:30 pm and 8:00 am, except for you sleeping at your desk," his boss said in a clearly pitiful tone. "What did you do?" And as he finished saying that, he turned his gaze to a monitor on the wall.

Jeff saw himself on that monitor, just as the director had explained seconds earlier. The clock on the bottom left of the screen was at 10:37 pm and it was still moving forward.

"Oh my god, this is good," Jeff thought to himself, "not only have I landed myself in a big mess, but I also appear guilty to the rest of the world."

He rose from his chair and approached the monitor. Instinctively he felt that this was not at all possible. Nothing made sense anymore. Not what had happened to him last night nor any of the things that happened to him since.

He looked at the small reflection of a LED light in the cup that was right in front of him on the recording. This LED in theory justified the activity of the network on a computer. It is absolutely impossible, under normal conditions, to be on or off for periods longer than one second at a time. The activity of the network normally made it blink vigorously. But there it was quietly and consistently burning without so much as a blink.

He stood back about a yard from the screen and could see that it was very difficult to discern that tiny green dot. He came closer again and saw that it was still there, burning consistently without any flickering. It was not conclusive proof, but he was sure that analyzing the security tape on the right equipment would confirm his theory.

He sat down again and tried to explain himself, recounting what he had already told Rose in private. This time he told his story in a much more comprehensive manner including every detail he remembered. When he had finished, he rose again pointing at the small reflection of the LED in the cup and said:

"I know it's hard to explain. This green dot reflecting in the cup might be invisible from where you are but it is the reflection of the LED of my terminal indicating the activity of the network. It should be blinking consistently, but it is impossible to keep it burning. During the minute I was here next to this monitor I didn't see it blink once, just like I don't see it blinking now. I am 100% sure that this video is a loop that someone has set up to make us believe that I was in the same position all night and that no one else intervened."

Both were intrigued with Jeff's explanation. His boss was clearly interested. He allowed him to finish his theory without interrupting once. When Jeff had finished his speech, there was a silence of nearly a minute. His boss, visibly impressed, said:

"Okay, Jeff, I believe you. Let us approach this matter with the highest confidentiality. Who else knows about all this apart from those present here now."

They both looked at each other for a moment, then turned their faces to their boss and said almost in unison:

"Nobody else"

They agreed that it was time to establish an urgent contingency plan. The crisis cabinet would be made up of the three of them, but they needed to involve somebody from security as well.

Linda was discarded almost immediately because she had been on duty the night before. She could be involved in some way. Charles's name came up almost spontaneously. Rose mentioned that she had to go back to him to return the surveillance tape. Returning the tape would be an opportune time to involve him in the matter.

In any case, the three agreed not to divulge more information than was absolutely necessary. For the moment, he would only be told that they had detected an incident on the surveillance system and that the best way to stop it was to keep it under wraps and try to catch the culprit red handed.

It seemed to Jeff that his boss was taking the unfolding events in his stride. When faced with a sensitive crisis like this it would be easy to lose one's temper or make harsh remarks but he stayed calm and composed. Jeff thought that the company really couldn't have made a better appointment for the State of New York even though his boss was not always as collected as he appeared today. Even the best of them would find working for that company challenging. It appeared as if this man had an inborn charisma to handle difficult situations with aplomb.

Jeff left, not entirely convinced that they were going to make much progress with those measures, but he was relieved that someone superior to him now knew the facts of all that had happened to him during the last few hours.The very thoughts that were still tormenting him.

He was determined that within the next 24 hours they would be able to make ample progress with their investigation. Surely they will know more than they knew now.

As events unfolded later, he would come to realize that he could not have been more wrong.

They parted ways in the hall. Jeff went back to his desk and Rose to the security office to return the tape and involve Charles in the investigation. Under different circumstances everything that was going on with Rose would have bothered him. The revelations Charles made to him a while ago did not sit well with him, but he had no time now to mull about that. He had to focus on what was really important.

Still in deep thought, he took a seat at his desk with the intention to start some constructive work for the day. He did not really know where to start or what to do. The disturbing events of the last couple of hours clouded his focus and entirely disrupted his routine, preventing him from doing the job he was paid to do.

6. Threats

[4:48pm]
At exactly 4:48 pm, his desk phone rang with it's usual shrill noise. With an absent "Jeff speaking" he invited the caller to speak.

"Listen closely, Jeff," said an intimidating, undoubtedly male voice, on the other side of the line, "We've been watching you since...," he paused, "the incident," he finished ominously.

Jeff tried his best to pick up some voice masking device on the other side, but all seemed normal.

"Yes," Jeff said nonchalantly, "And... ?"

"Stop poking your nose into this. Tomorrow at midnight all will be over and everything will be back to normal. I warn you, if you keep on meddling, someone close to you will pay," With these words, he hung up the receiver, leaving Jeff listening to the monotonous beep beep beep on the phone.

It took him a moment to realise the gravity of what just happened . He didn't expect to be left with more questions than answers. Pensively, he hung up the receiver and allowed his imagination to wander, inventing different scenarios. At least his doubts about the plot was laid to rest. It was now all too obvious. He had to discuss it with the team. But it was necessary to first solve two pressing matters in this equation. Firstly, who were the people behind all this, and secondly who did the caller refer to when he mentioned someone close to him.

He hardly had any friends in that huge metropolis and his family all remained in his hometown. Sometimes he could clearly recall the smell of his mother's stew and the quiet streets in the early evenings of May, when the trees were in full bloom and the scent of flowers filled his lungs. The comfort in knowing that after his walk, the longed-for stew would be waiting on the table at home.

His brain worked overtime to the point of cracking his skull. Finally he came to the conclusion that the caller must have meant Rose. She was by far the most important person to him in this big city.

Feeling quite sure that he clarified that point for himself, his thoughts wandered on to the next question. Who could be behind all this and why? It was obvious that it was related to the client whom he was working for but it all made no sense. Who would do that and why go to that much trouble?

The voice of the caller was not of much help either. There was not the slightest hint of any emotion in that voice. He wondered whether it could have been a recording, but the interaction appeared too natural. He remembered a course he did at the agency where one rehearsed some text with a colleague over the phone for days. Eventually it became so monotonous and mechanical almost to the point of sounding robotic. He was simply the messenger conveying a message. To make things harder with each repetition, his partner would ask unscripted questions or interrupt in mid sentence.

He looked down at his desk trying to focus on reality again. He took a blank sheet of paper from the drawer and started drawing an organizational chart. He knew that the web job he was doing for the client was sourced and came directly from his supervisor, Daniel. He once overheard him saying that the job was allocated to the company through a colleague. At that moment he couldn't remember who it was, but he knew exactly where he could find it: on the net.

He started by looking up new images related to EADAR and scrolled through pages and pages filled with numerous pictures. On page seventeen a face caught his eye. He clicked with the mouse on the image to enlarge it. It became bigger and he noticed that the image was taken from the personal blog of a lesser known journalist. If he was well known it would have been on one of the first pages. That is how search algorithms work, he thought.

He clicked on the image again and the browser took him directly to the blog where the photo of the man appeared. After a brief review of the article, which barely took him 15 seconds (he was accustomed to reading such things in that time or less), he came to the conclusion that the person he was looking for was Charles Smith, a well-known investor who was behind some of the most disruptive startups that the city has seen in recent months. It was a kind of *business angel.*

He wrote down the name on the page and finished the flow chart by placing a box with an X on one side and linking it to both the customer and Mr. Smith.

[5:30pm]
He folded the paper carefully and slipped it into the pocket of his shirt. He looked around through the windows that opened to other offices, the rest of his colleagues seemed to be hard at work and nobody noticed what he had just done. How he hated being in the middle of the corridor! He got up and went back to the 42nd floor, not without first going around to the reception hall and giving Rose a conspiratorial look. She left her desk as soon as she could, and also headed to the elevator.

When Rose arrived at the chief's office, Jeff was already briefing the chief on the latest developments: the call, the discovery of who was involved, and especially the person Jeff believed might be in danger in case of not following their instructions. For this reason, the three decided to yet again pretend that the meeting was about work. The chief picked up the phone and called his secretary.

"Just play along," he told them both.

The voluptuous secretary, burst into the office flooding the room with her Chanel number five. Jeff could not avoid rubbing his nose. Strong smells, even pleasant ones, often overwhelmed him. He did not remember the secretary, but that was not strange either.

It was a strenuous and very demanding job to be the secretary for the big boss and as far as he could remember there had been quite a few over the past few years. He also didn't go up to the executive floor very often. They were on that floor removed from the rest for a reason...

The secretary approached the table and sat down in a nearby chair, which seemed to be her usual spot. She put the notepad on the edge of the desk and put the tips of her high-heeled shoes together with exquisite delicacy. Jeff gawked at the ritual. The chief's voice took him out of his reverie.

"Take note," the chief said in his accustomed distant tone.

"To the Human Resources Department, colon, Jeff Patterson is relieved of his current duties and temporarily moved to the reserve team until further notice. His position will be filled by whomever Daniel Roberts decides to designate to the role. Deliver this order immediately."

The secretary left the room the same way she entered. She picked up her notepad and her pen, pulled back the chair carefully and headed for the door, leaving a trail of perfume behind her.

"Take care, Jeff, I hope you get better soon," said the boss so the secretary could hear it clearly.

Once she closed the door, the conversation resumed.

"All right. Go home now, but first visit a phone shop and buy two phones with disposable cards. Send a bouquet and a box of chocolates to Rose with a courier. Put one of the phones inside the box and keep her updated on all developments. From now on: no emails, conventional phone calls or anything that could link you to this job", said the chief.

"Understood Boss. I suppose Rose will report directly to you?"

"No, not if we don't have to. The less comings and goings to this office the better. We will check in every three hours. Rose will come up here and we'll have a conference on the disposable phones," the boss snapped.

"Okay, I think it's perfect. I'm leaving immediately," Jeff said, "As for the client... I think someone should talk to Daniel..."

"No, forget about all that now. Besides, technically you're out. Jeff, proceed with caution. And above all, act as if you were really on vacation."

And with that last remark they ended the meeting. It was clear that things were truly complicated. It was important to follow the plan carefully. If he was right, Rose's life was in danger. They set it up to create the impression that he was no longer linked to the case in any way, leaving the extortionists free to continue with whatever they were doing without any obstacles.

They were silent walking down the corridor and taking the lift back to their respective workplaces. Both of them were completely overwhelmed by recent events. Jeff because he feared Rose might be in grave danger because of him and Rose because the gravity of the situation finally hit her. The threat that Jeff revealed a few minutes ago in the chief's office left her feeling very vulnerable.

[6:04pm]
Back in the reception area they parted with a simple "Take care". She returned to her work station and he went back to his desk to switch off the computer and clear his desk to make it look as if he was actually leaving the company for a few days.

Now more than ever he had to be very cautious.

He felt very troubled and the signs of weariness was obvious in his gait towards the lift. The doorman greeted when he passed, but he was so absorbed that he did not hear his greeting.

He still had to make the purchases they agreed upon. A couple of blocks away were a couple of electronics and appliance stores where he knew he could get anything from cameras to cell phones. He wandered towards that street with all the recent events still mulling in his head. Without realizing it he arrived in front of one of the stores.

He walked into the store and asked for disposable phones. The clerk, eager to make a sale in an area of vibrant competition, asked a few prudent questions and returned almost right away with two phones.

"Do they work?"

"Definitely Sir, we pride ourselves in the quality of our products. We can try them here if that would set your mind at ease," the clerk said.

After testing the phones to verify that both of them worked and were able to make and receive calls, he took out his wallet and put two bills on the counter.

The clerk thought it was his lucky day. No haggling or ludicrous demands. It was not what he was used to, but such a welcome change! He took the money from the counter and handed the two phones to Jeff in a plastic bag.

He still had to get the flowers and chocolates. He knew it was probably better to buy it in Manhattan than in his neighbourhood as it was likely that the prices there would be less, but the variety here was certainly better. He turned the corner and headed for a less commercial area.

He passed a gift shop and bought a box of chocolates. Before leaving the street, he emptied the contents in a wastebasket and put one of the cell phones in its place.

Things seemed to go according to plan. Finally, he had to get the flowers. He had no idea right now where in that area he might find a florist, but trusting in his fate, he continued walking without a definite course.

He came across a flower shop on the way. He surely did not frequent flower shops, but if he did he might still have been with Rose.

The sheer variety of shapes and colors displayed in the window made his head spin. In his mind he conjured up an image of Rose receiving one of those exquisite bouquets and smiled in approval. It was as if the show he was putting on was in fact part of something real.

Inside, a very vivacious employee guided him in choosing a bouquet of red roses on the pretext that to conquer a lady there is nothing better. He could not help but appreciate something personal in the treatment he received. For some unexplained reason it seemed to him that this young woman might be in the same situation as himself.

He filled out a gift card with good wishes and gave the delivery address to the young shop assistant before paying for the bouquet.

He re-read what he had written:

Rose: I've taken a few days off. I'm a bit overwhelmed at work and also need to think about us. I still feel the same way about you. Please forgive me that I did not tell you this in person and accept these flowers and chocolates as a sign of my love.

Jeff

He knew that although the note was a total invention, it contained a lot of truth. He still harboured strong and intense feelings for Rose. After all, it was she who decided to end the relationship. He wondered if she would be able to read between the lines beyond the scope of his instructions. He surely hoped so.

With Rose you never knew: she was methodical and calculating. He knew she liked romantic gestures, but could be ridiculously pragmatic sometimes. Jeff on the other hand was impulsive and liked to surprise her by doing crazy things like booking tickets to watch a movie in another state because it would premiere there first. She of course would have none of that as they needed to travel hundreds of miles for it. Even though she had her little quirks like that, he should have showed his love for her more often by surprising her with roses from time to time. But all that is water under the bridge now.

[6:56pm]
The long walk and effort of all the shopping left him a bit tired with no inclination whatsoever to take the underground back home. Without thinking twice, he raised his hand and flagged down a taxi.

Fortunately Manhattan taxi drivers were not at all chatty like the ones would encounter in Spain who simply love to make small talk with all their passengers. He fondly remembered all the chats he had in Madrid with the taxi drivers whisking him around the city. They didn't really care whether or not you could even speak Spanish, they just chattered along passing the time. The peace and quiet inside this taxi allowed him to focus on his own affairs now.

He stood on the landing of the stairs staring at the keyhole as if that would open the door as if by magic. Finally he took the key from his right pocket, unlocked the door and stepped inside.

He set the alarm on his cell phone for one hour and chucked it on the couch. He did not want to fall asleep but he needed to think about what was happening and what his next step should be. Again thoughts of Rose drifted into his mind. The times they were together at the movies or a concert. So many happy memories. He dwelled on their visit to Liberty Island. Holding hands, circling the Statue of Liberty. The cold air was more intense there as there were no buildings to shelter them from the nasty wind. It was such a good day. They walked hand in hand, saw wonderful things and talked for hours.

[8:11pm]
The alarm from the cell phone brought him back to reality. He looked at the time and calculated that the dealer would have made the delivery. He picked up the disposable cell phone and called the other number, following the plan. This call was not strictly agreed upon but he wanted to check that everything was in place and working according to plan.

After two rings, the phone was picked up but he did not hear the expected invitation to speak.

"Rose?" said Jeff.

After a couple of awkward seconds...

"Jeff, we told you not to interfere, you have put the life of your partner in danger. She is fine...," he said as if to take a breath, "for now. If you behave and stop meddling, we will release her tomorrow night at twelve," he hung up abruptly.

How could it be? He felt totally trapped. Less than two hours ago they made the perfect plan in the chief's office. Only the three people present in that office knew the details of the plan and now, at this shattering moment it appeared that whoever was behind all this had the upper hand. They were definitely smarter and better prepared or...

Yes, that had to be it. There was someone fully aware of their plan and two steps ahead of them... "There is a mole", he whispered to himself. But how will he find out who it is? All the information seemingly known by the extortioner was only known to the three of them, or was it...?

He went to the kitchen and took a piece of paper and a pen. He started making a list of the suspects.

By the time he wrote down a dozen names he realised that it was all in vain. Surely the person he was looking for was not on that list, or if he was there were too many names on the list to rule out anyone in such a short time. He had to come to some conclusion within the hour, as the danger to Rose was increasing with every second that passed.

Something had to be done, and fast. He began sifting and discarding possibilities in his head while trying not to lose sight of the list at the same time. He tried weighing up more than one possibility at once as he was taught in the agency. He was subjected to numerous tests of unfolded thinking and was believed to be one of only a few minds able to perform that exercise successfully.

He managed to keep it up for 127 seconds on one occasion. The test consisted of keeping count of numbers with a certain pattern while at the same time memorizing a list of words that were appearing on a screen. To establish the validity of the test, the training would last for weeks memorizing lists and reciting numbers out loud following a certain pattern.

The exercise ended when the number sequence was broken. He would then immediately proceed to recite the memorized words. Each word had a time stamp from the time it was flashed on the screen. So his record actually meant that he was able to memorize about fifty words while reciting the alternate prime numbers. A normal brain would need about one second for each word, but he was only given half a second per word.

There was something on the list that stirred in the back of his mind. He could clearly see that someone on the inside had to be involved. He needed to debug the list. Devise a little test that would allow him to lure the damned mole from its hiding place.

But no matter how hard he tried, he could not come up with anything that could be useful in this case. In addition, he ran the risk of getting a false positive.

[8:40pm]
He again fell asleep on the couch trying to get clarity on what

was happening. When he finally woke up and saw the time on his cell phone he gave a shocked gasp. He knew he had lost a lot of sleep, but now was not the time to catch up on that. He washed his face and put on a clean shirt. When he felt less groggy, he picked up his things and opened the door to leave.

[9:16am]
He went down to the street and entered a rather popular hotel around the corner. He sat down at the bar and ordered a mint tea. He opened the bag of sugar gingerly and poured it into the cup very carefully. Though his eyes were fixed on the little grains of sweetness falling into the cup, he did not really see them.

He was so deeply absorbed in his thoughts that he kept the envelope in the same position for quite a while after it was already empty. When he realized it, he put the envelope aside, picked up the spoon and stirred the drink rhythmically as if each turn of the spoon would energize his mind. Much like the cranks used in the olden days to start motor vehicles.

This rhythm continued for several minutes. Suddenly he stopped stirring, brought the edge of the cup to his lips and swallowed the contents in a single gulp. He left a five dollars bill next to the cup and left the establishment. He made his way to the main avenue...

7. The trojan

Time was of the essence now and his mind worked overtime. Within seconds he decided to work alone without the involvement of anyone as no one could be trusted.

"Beth," said to himself.

Beth had been his close companion during college. They were a perfect match on so many levels and even became lovers at some point. It was a very intense relationship but it didn't last long because their personalities proved to be too similar.

Beth was truly brilliant. She was currently working as *break-breach* for a company linked to the public sector as far as he could remember. (*break-breach: A specialist who tries to break into, usually in a fraudulent way, third-party computer systems. In this case Beth performs those functions but to assess the risk and critical vulnerabilities in the systems she analyzes.*)

He did not know whether the phone number he had for her would still be working, but he had to try.

"Wait a moment," said to himself. "So far they have been one step ahead all of the time. It would be foolish to call her without taking some precautions and most definitely not in the street where someone was probably watching him."

He walked back to the bar where he enjoyed the mint tea a few minutes earlier and went straight to the restroom, locked himself in one of the cubicles, and sat down on the toilet bowl. He scrolled through his contacts until Beth's profile appeared on the screen. Jeff paused a few seconds to consider all the possibilities before making the call. There were definitely cameras and hidden microphones in his work place, of that he was sure. His phone could be tapped and then it wouldn't really matter where he made the call.

All the complications he was facing reminded him of a scene from a movie he saw several times. He rummaged through the folds of his weary brain and grimaced at how difficult he found it to remember everyday things. When he wrote programs, in what may seem to be indecipherable gibberish to an outsider, he was at full tilt though. He blinked and returned to reality.

Finally he put down the phone. He rose slowly as if the indecision of his brain involuntary slowed down his movements .

[9:51am]
He saw a coat hanging on the clothes rack at the entrance to the toilets and realised that there was someone else in one of the other stalls. Without much thought he slipped his hand into one of the inside pockets and pulled out a smartphone. He tried to unlock the screen and "Bingo!", he sighed relieved when the phone granted him access.

The owner of the mobile obviously neglected to install any security mechanism and the phone allowed him to choose an application. He walked out and into the adjacent toilet for disabled people. He knew that he could lock the door from the inside and thus have some privacy.

Hurriedly he dialed Beth's number and started the call. His heart was racing faster with every ring and he was unsure that she would even answer the phone when she sees an unknown number.

On the fourth ring the phone was picked up and he heard her familiar voice.

"Beth here".

"Hi Beth, it's Jeff, I don't know if you remember me."

"Jeff?" and two seconds later, "of course! Just kidding. How could I forget you! How long has it been? I am quite busy at the moment though..."

"I have to see you urgently. It's a matter of life or death! I've managed to pilfer this cell phone to call you," he said in a desperate tone.

"Alright: in one hour at our bar. Get rid of the cell phone," she said firm.

"Oh my god, I didn't remember her quite so decisive and efficient! Obviously the many years of hacking security systems to establish their safety levels have hardened her", he thought. Our bar. He fondly remembered their meetings after class in the bar on the corner of 7th Avenue and 57th Street. They spent hours there going over algorithms and sharing stories.

There was not much time to get to the bar. It was quite a few subway stops away and he realised that he would probably need to take a taxi to make it on time.

Before leaving, he needed to erase his tracks on the borrowed phone. He went to the phone settings and restored it to the default factory settings. It was definitely going to cause a terrible inconvenience to the owner, but he could not afford to leave any tracks. At least he was returning the phone and not getting rid of it in the toilet bowl.

He hurried back to the main toilet and inserted the cell phone into the same pocket of the jacket where he found it. Apparently the owner had severe intestinal problems as he was still in the restroom.

Coming out of the bar he gave a whistle followed by screaming 'Taxi!"

A yellow car stopped and he said to the driver before getting in: "To the Apple Store on fifth Avenue", in a tone loud enough to make it clear where he was going if someone was listening.

He got into the car and after two blocks said to the taxi driver: "Excuse me, a change of plans. Rather take me to the corner of seventh avenue and fifty-seventh street."

The taxi driver, clearly grumpy about this sudden change, changed lanes to alter his course. Jeff turned his head and could see from of the corner of his eye how a black sedan switched lanes at the same time, about four cars behind them.

"Shit," said to himself.

"Fifty extra bucks if you let me make a call with your cell phone," he told the driver.

The driver rummaged through the glove compartment and produced a rather old Nokia phone.

"No idea if it has enough battery left to call," he said.

Jeff could not believe that there were still people using these ancient flip phones. Too grateful, he kept his comments to himself. The driver already seemed rather irritated to risk provoking him any further. He called Beth again, this time by heart. Jeff found it very easy to remember numbers and this one he saw only a few minutes ago.

"Beth," he said, as he leaned against the window to try and stay out of sight of the taxi driver as well as the car following them, "they are following me," he continued.

"Ok, go to a public place, and I will meet you there. Any ideas?"

"What about the Apple Store of the fifth Avenue? Would that be ok for you?" Jeff said to her.

"Seems perfect. 10:30 there." She hung up.

"Sir, please forgive me, but I actually need to go to the Apple store now. My phone is definitely broken," he said.

"Well," he said in a markedly disgusted tone, "what about my cell phone?"

"I'm really quite desperate. Instead of 50 bucks for the call I just made... I'll give you 200 for the cell phone, the card and the charger," he said in a serious tone of voice.

"500 and it's all yours," the taxi driver said, thinking he was making a great deal.

"Three hundred and the trip is included. I don't have more money on me."

The taxi driver, knowing a good deal when he sees it, put out his hand waiting for the money. Jeff pulled out his wallet and said, "I'll give it to you on arrival," and showed him the notes in the rearview mirror.

He laid back in the seat and allowed his thoughts to drift to Beth.

During their years at University they went to several recitals and concerts and he suddenly remembered a specific night and classical music recital.

The violin solo of the Adagio in G by Albinoni gave him goose bumps with its serene beauty. He closed his eyes and touched her hand. If it had not been for the feeling of sadness that filled him when he heard that melody, it might well have been the happiest moment of his life. The music filled him with such awe that the melody mulled around in his head for weeks after that. He eventually ended up buying himself a violin and entering private music lessons for adults.

He then felt very close to his hero, Sherlock Holmes. Although to be fair, he had to practice and practice to even get a glimmer of ever becoming a virtuoso.

He returned to reality when the taxi driver took him out of his daydream. They had arrived.

[10:22am]

After paying the agreed amount, he walked quietly to the entrance of the store and began to descend the staircase with unusual care. The sheer number of people who visited this place allowed him to go unnoticed.

He was literally going down step by step watching from the corner of his eye for possible followers. They were very good because he couldn't see anyone suspicious but he was convinced they were there.

His angle on the spiral staircase and the slow descent allowed him to survey the shop much more closely than usual. In the past he was always in a rush when he visited the shop. It seemed to be much bigger than he remembered. The absence of pillars and the flood of natural light through the enormous glass cube up top gave the space a supernatural feel. The inspiration derived from the Louvre in Paris was evident in the huge glass structure with the bitten apple.

When he reached the lower floor he went straight to the accessories department and began to browse around in the most carefree way he could manage without losing sight of the access stairs to the store. Within minutes he spotted an out of place couple in black suits and dark sunglasses. It was all too clear to him: they did follow him.

It would be impossible to dodge them. There was only one exposed exit via the stairs . He realised that it was a grave mistake to choose that shop for the meeting.

"Hi, Jeff, it's me, don't turn yet" a subdued voice said next to him.

"Good day Sir, how can I help you?" the voice continued now perfectly normal and quite audible. He turned around and could hardly contain his surprise when he saw Beth.

"I have this…," he stammered, "old phone," showing her the old phone he just bought from the cab driver, "and I would like to upgrade to a more modern one, but I'd like to keep the number.

It is very important to me. A friend of mine has this number and I hope to get a call."

"Well, let me see, I can offer you the latest iPhone model, but we will have to cut out the SIM card and I don't know if yours will allow it. Some old models have contacts outside the area that will be trimmed away," said Beth convincingly.

One of the men in black was close enough to overhear the whole conversation, while pretending to be trying an iPad distractedly.

"Excuse me a moment. I will take the phone to the technical team to find out if it is possible to cut this card as I explained."

She took the phone from him, brushing his hand lightly with the tips of her fingers. That was Beth's way of infusing courage. This had helped him many times in the past to calm down before an examination.

As Beth disappeared through the door into the back office, Jeff again looked distractedly at accessories, trying not to lose sight of the men in black.

Beth was back at his side after only ten minutes.

"The technical department confirmed that it will be possible to convert your SIM into a nano-sim, but you have to authorize it with this document," she said and handed him an official Apple form. It is very important that you read and understand the terms and conditions carefully. Sometimes the process is quite complicated and you could lose some of your contacts." she said professionally and allowed him time to read.

Jeff immediately noticed the small print on the the document:

I accept the conversion of SIM card number OORITHBWFINK967 and understand that stored data or contacts might be lost.

"That's odd!" he thought. "Beth would not have insisted that I read the terms and conditions if there was nothing to see." He looked at the form again but saw nothing out of the ordinary. The only thing that stood out was the number of the SIM but he could not verify it.

He suddenly remembered the key they used to encrypt things at the university. The serial number was the only suspect item on the form and he began transposing that to see if it contained some hidden message. After a few moments he saw in his mind's eye above the serial number: **2:30pmrudysgrill**.

He remembered that place well: pitchers of beer, hotdogs, and a jukebox. On 9th Avenue between 44th and 45th streets.

He signed the document and handed it back to her.

"It will take ten minutes to process the card," she said as she invited him to follow her.

"Tell me, which model were you considering?"

[10:51am]
The rest of the interaction occurred quite naturally and business-like. He chose an iPhone and took it with the sim card he bought from the taxi driver, now converted to fit in the new instrument.

[11:12am]
On the way home he received a couple of calls which he did not answer. He didn't know how he was going to keep the appointment and prevent them from following him again. Maybe if he disguised himself... He thought about his childhood and the Halloween costumes that varied between the grotesque and the hilarious. His group of friends always fiercely contested who could come up with the most disgusting disguise.

[12:07am]
He opened the closet and looked for something elegant. He did not really wear suits but remembered that he kept one or two from previous events his company hosted in the past. Events that he was forced to attend and for which almost all employees dressed up.

He shaved his beard, leaving only a small moustache and goatee. He looked through the drawers and retrieved glasses he had not used in a long time, since he had undergone laser surgery for myopia..

He tried several hairstyles. He left the parting in the middle but that seemed too hipster and that was not the look he was going for. Then he combed his hair back with some water but that made him look too young.

When he thought he had tried everything, he found some grease in one of the drawers. He smeared the thick liquid from root to tip on his hair and left it disheveled, giving him a modern yet casual style. If he came out of all this alive, it could be a good look for future parties and events.

Although his appearance had changed considerably, he did not want to risk being recognized at the entrance of his building. He was sure that they knew where he lived. He put on a trenchcoat and walked toward the back of the building. He started down the emergency stairs carefully.

When he reached the ground, he looked both ways and raised the collar of the raincoat to cover his face as much as possible. He walked towards the avenue opposite the main entrance of his building and raised his hand to call a taxi.

[2:28pm]
The taxi dropped him right at the door of the bar. The big man at the entrance grimaced as if authorizing his passage. Just as well because his ID photo did not match his current look. Despite these rudimentary controls, minors nevertheless managed to sneak into places with alcohol. He entered directly without looking around. On his left the long bar ended in a small corner and to his right there were two large tables with chairs. Although his new look was good, he did not want to risk being caught by drawing attention to himself. In addition, if viewed from the front, it was much easier to recognize him.

He approached the bottom of the bar where there were some free spots. Moments after sitting down, Beth appeared on the scene and sat next to him. She kissed him on the cheek. The touch of her soft lips on his freshly shaved face caused a barrage of memories of their college days. He suppressed those memories right away. He could not afford any distractions now.

They ordered a jug of lager beer. They knew it would be accompanied by some hot dogs. He was hungry and could not remember when last he had a bite to eat.

He was very curious and asked her about her current job and how she managed to serve him at the Apple store.

"I work sporadically in that store, not more than four hours a week," she told him, "It allows me to be much better at my real work. I had to call in a favor to be able to serve you not to mention the forms that I gave you, but we'll talk about that later."

Jeff briefed her on everything that had happened to him in the last few hours. He was getting tired of having to repeat the whole mess again and again. That was the third time he had to talk about it in detail and he hoped it was the last. Even so, Beth was not to blame for that, so he tried to explain in a detailed and friendly way.

After he finished his take on the whole complicated story, they exchanged ideas on the best course of action to solve the situation. Beth proposed something in which she happened to be an expert. Her idea was to introduce a program into the system that would allow them to control the transactions that were taking place.

They agreed on the procedure to follow: Beth would be in charge of creating a *trojan* that would enter the system by clicking on the URL that Beth would send in a normal advertising email. Once the Trojan was in operation it would be a matter of a few hours to counteract the effects of the funds transfers that caused the breach. During that time Jeff and Beth would devote all their time and efforts to locating Rose.

[3:46pm]
All the efforts he made to go unnoticed and escape the eyes of the watchers seemed to have been effective. He decided to disregard the chief's explicit orders and go back to the office. In truth his disguise and "new character" would make it impossible for him to enter the office, so once in the taxi he started to get rid of things to become recognisable again.

He took off the spectacles which has made him quite dizzy. Since the operation for myopia years ago he has never worn them again. He didn't really know why he kept them as he was not a particularly sentimental person. Be that as it may, they came in quite handy today. Jeff tried to get his hair back to normal by using both hands to undo the effect of the grease as best he could. Luckily he had the foresight to put a disposable razor in his pocket which he now used to dry shave the moustache and goatee. It would just appear as if he decided to shave his beard off completely.

[4:39pm]
When he arrived at the huge glass tower where his company had its headquarters, the guard at the entrance told him:

"What have you done, Jeff? You look quite different ..."

"I've shaved my beard, Tom. I was a little fed up with it," he tried to say as nonchalantly as he could.

The usual elevator ride took him to his floor. When he arrived at his desk he began to check documentation and pretended to work, not to arouse suspicion. The location of his workplace in the hallway did not suit him at all.

Meanwhile, elsewhere in Manhattan

With her glasses on the table, the chair slightly leaning backwards and a small cup of steaming coffee beside her, Beth leaned back cupping her neck with her hands, smiling happily.

Her thoughts wandered back all those years to the University campus where she met Jeff.

At first he seemed a typical nerd. As time went by she realized that he was sensitive, detailed, intelligent and...nice. Unlike any man she has known before.

They immediately hit it off and one thing led to another. By the end of the semester they were inseparable. Still lulled in happiness she sipped her coffee and then started to work. She liked to believe that fate brought Jeff back to her and this time she will be more careful not to lose him again. If he didn't feel the same, he was still a very good friend in serious trouble. If only for that reason she had to do her best for him.

During her years in this tough and competitive profession she earned herself quite a reputation for being too demanding, especially with those around her. So much so that she usually worked alone. Not many people could keep up with her high standards nor did they want to.

She was conscientious, methodical and very intelligent. She knew exactly what to do about the problem at Jeff's company. Someone had set up a program that transferred funds on a regular basis.

All she had to do was install a gateway to gain access and her program would do the rest: counteract the function of the malware, if it was still possible. Her work usually began by installing a trojan that would allow her access.

She had a part-time job at a telephony company to provide the necessary cover and allow her access to a few email accounts that she could use to install her Trojan appearing to be legitimate communications.

She used a two pronged approach: sending a link per email and when clicked upon the Trojan would be installed during the redirection.

In Jeff's case she was tempted to send the file directly which would enable her to install it from the terminal on the server.

For some reason she decided against that and thought it more appropriate to follow the normal procedure and avoid involving Jeff more than necessary, should something go wrong. In addition she found it perversely satisfying to outwit the security system, almost like experiencing an orgasm.

A case came to mind where she had to disguise herself as a food distributor, hiding the trojan on a CD which was handed out with the food as part of a welcome package. It was quite a challenge to make a CD that looked commercial enough as to not raise suspicions.

[5:12pm]
She carefully prepared the email that would carry the link. Normally she would study the targets carefully to make the mail credible. They should have complete confidence to click on the link without even thinking about it.

In general it was not too difficult to obtain the data necessary to give credibility to the mail. Most of the executives and technical workers from her target companies have complete profiles on one or more of the most used social networks.

She was able to have a complete record of the subject in question within minutes. In addition, the trick of offering irresistible cell phone deals always worked like a charm. Who would not be interested to see what better deals the competition to one's current provider had on offer?

It was not really necessary to go to such lengths with Jeff as she was sure he would follow the link as instructed. However, she did not want to leave any room for suspicion as emails are usually archived and she had to cover her tracks.

After reviewing the mail again and checking that the link was correct, she clicked the send button. She knew she would not have to wait long before getting the answer from the system. She opened the monitoring program and took a sip of coffee, which she immediately spat into her cup as it was already cold.

She got up to make a new cup of coffee when, halfway to the kitchen, a ping sounded on the computer. The alarm would sound when the monitoring program detected activity. She turned around to check what triggered the alarm. It could only be Jeff. She went back to the terminal to start her magic.

Meanwhile at Jeff's office...

[6:01pm]
It had not even been ninety minutes when Jeff received a notice on his cell that he had mail to download. Upon entering the company he configured his email to be available on his mobile to alert him to urgent messages that needed his attention. Naively he thought it might earn him some points with his direct boss, Daniel. The reality was somewhat different though. Once he was overzealous and disturbed Daniel after hours on a matter he considered urgent, but was suitably reprimanded. After that he lost interest and uninstalled the email account from his personal mobile.

For this occasion he reconfigured it to stay abreast of Beth's progress. He opened the email application and waited for the list of messages to display. The only one that was unread, came from an unknown sender. He opened it and could see that it had Beth's signature all over it:

```
Dear user, we tried to get hold of you on the num-
bers you provided at the time of registration, wi-
thout success.
We would like to offer you an excellent deal. Plea-
se check the link below for the details of the offer.
http://www.redirect.com/?id=12jkd98

B.S.
```

There was no doubt that the message came from Beth. As he read each sentence he could imagine Beth typing it. She always had an uncanny talent for this kind of thing. He remembered an incident when they wanted to pull a prank on one of the teachers and Beth was assigned the project. She prepared documents so legit that not even an expert would have suspected otherwise.

All he had to do was open the email on his desktop computer, click on the link provided and the plan will be set into action. After clicking on the link he noticed a slight forwarding action and a small icon that was installed on the navigation bar. He realised that under normal circumstances the forwarding and the icon would go completely unnoticed unless you were really very observant.

Now all he had to do was wait. He knew Beth would already be aware that he had followed the link as agreed.

It was therefore unnecessary to warn her.

8. False hopes

In order to avoid suspicion, the trojan worked inside the operating system and was tracking all the movement of funds. It was then stored and delayed for as long as possible to prevent any further loss of money. This could give them a window of three hours to try and locate Rose.

In their respective offices both of them were pondering the question of where to begin their search. They agreed to limit their contact to the minimum to avoid detection and only use the phone Jeff bought from the taxi driver. The bulk of the contact happened via text messages, although they made the odd call when necessary.

They were relatively sure that the disposable phone Jeff sent with the flowers would be where Rose was held. The hijackers probably expected him to make contact in order to find out whether she was still alive. Even so, that theory might not be true and only lulled them into the false belief that they had a tactical advantage.

Both of them knew that time was of the essence and they had to act fast even though chances of success were remote. It was their only shot at finding Rose. Beth set up a device that would triangulate the position of the cell phone to within a radius of 10 meters, provided the phone was switched on of course. Then the phone should also ring for at least 10 seconds or a conversation should be carried on for the same time at least to be able to locate the position.

As they did not have many other options available to them, they decided to give it their best shot. They agreed via text message on the exact time Jeff was to call Rose's disposable phone. Beth would then try to figure out the location of the phone with the triangulation device.

A few minutes before the prearranged time, Jeff suddenly felt overwhelmed and began to sweat. He had enormous doubts about what they were about to do. For some strange reason he began to doubt himself and thought he should rather have involved the police.

He often experienced similar situations when he worked for the agency. These levels of stress really wrecked havoc on one's body. The adrenaline was pumping and he was overcome by fear. As he was taught then, he began to take deep breaths and tried to focus on the issue at hand rather than the consequences of it.

At the agreed time he managed to compose himself. He realized they were Rose's only hope of survival. He flipped the cell phone open and pressed the key 1 to access the quick memory of the last number dialed. At first it did not ring as if the signal was too weak to make a call. He was about to hang up when he heard a slight click on the line.

"Is anyone there?," he asked in a worried tone.

There was no response. He could hear a faint sound on the line that reminded him of a potato fryer heard from a distance.

Suddenly he heard a loud blow of someone being hit and shouting voices in the distance which he couldn't quite make out.

"What a bitch! She was trying to talk on her cell phone!" Jeff could distinguish.

And then the line went dead and he could hear nothing. He was upset by what he had heard and wondered whether the line was open long enough for Beth to make the triangulation. He did not want to disturb her and was sure that if she had any news, she would get in touch. He was feeling deeply worried.

The sound of his mobile vibrating on the table quickly pulled him from his negative thoughts and he felt optimistic for a moment. He picked it up immediately, realizing it was Beth calling.

"Please tell me that everything went well..."

"Jeff... I don't know what exactly happened. I had the location for an instant but then lost it again. It was as if the earth swallowed the phone," she said concerned.

But you have the location, right ?

"Yes I do, but don't go alone. I'll pick you up. It's a very suspicious place. It appears in google maps as an abandoned building and the pedestrian view is not very encouraging," she told him without revealing the location.

"Okay, I'll meet you at my building's entrance," Jeff finished the call .

He went downstairs inmediately, knowing that Beth would take at least ten minutes to arrive, but he preferred to be outside in the fresh air rather than the confines of his desk in front of the computer. Furthermore, he did not want to make her wait. He paced up and down in front of the building like a caged animal in the zoo. If he had smoked in those few minutes, he would have consumed at least four or five cigarettes.

A voice from a taxi parked a few yards away pulled him out of his pacing routine and he hurried to get into the vehicle.

On the way to the address, Jeff took Beth's hand...in an unsure attempt to find relief or comfort. They were quiet during the trip. He was deeply worried and totally consumed by guilt. She knew full well the pressure he was under and remained silent. She knew he would speak if and when he was ready.

They arrived at the building and it was much worse than Beth imagined. It was a grimy, rat infested building smelling of urine.

They looked around for the entrance to the building but could only find an access hatch to the basement. Many buildings in New York had this ingenious system of space utilization. Jeff always thought a hole opening in the middle of the sidewalk to be a very dangerous concept.

Beth came prepared with a flashlight. They managed to open the latch and entered the building in the flashlight's dim beam. Working through the building they eventually found the place where they presumably held Rose for the last few hours. Or so it seemed at least.

In the middle of the damp and dirty room they found the remains of the disposable cell phone. It was obviously crushed by the large shoes of a very forceful man. The remains of the destroyed cell left no doubt that this must have been the place where Rose was kept.

They also saw a chair with ropes still hanging from it and a few drops of blood on the floor. It appeared to have splattered from a blow to the face. It was clear that Rose put up a fight and had to be restrained.

They were back to square one. In fact they were even worse off now as they had no further leads to go on. They had no means of communicating with Rose or the hijackers.

They decided that it was best to leave separately and each one took a taxi.

Elsewhere in Manhattan...

A black DMC van slows down between Dyer Avenue and 31st Street, opening its side door to chuck out a body like a bag of potatoes. As soon as it hit the ground the van sped off in the direction of the Lincoln tunnel and vanished from sight.

The first cars tried to get around the bound body in the middle of the road. It appeared to be a woman. At last one of the drivers stopped his vehicle, switching on the emergency lights. The first ambulance would only arrive on the scene more than eleven minutes later.

"She is not responding! We have to immobilize the spine and get her to hospital fast," the paramedic told the driver.

Within a few minutes they stabilised Rose on the scene, rushed her to the ambulance and sped away with howling sirens. In the back the medical staff worked frantically to monitor her vital signs. Her pulse was weak and fluttering. They intubated her trachea to help her breath. Apart from her prior injuries, the fall exacerbated her condition to a critical state.

And being tied up when she fell did not help either. She could not brace herself with her arms to soften the blow and injured vital organs. Her face and arms were also bruised and it was unsure whether she was even conscious when she was flung from the vehicle. It appeared to be the act of a criminal who just wanted to get rid of a body he considered to be dead already.

This was also the explanation Jeff received from Rose's sister when he went to see her at the hospital. Access to her room was restricted to family and staff only. Through the observation window he could see her fragile body on the bed, full of tubes and cables, linking her to monitors on both sides of the headboard.

The medical staff only spoke to the immediate family, so he had to settle for the report that her sister had given him.

He did not know what to think anymore. They threatened to harm someone close to him, and they did. They did it without him violating their instructions. It gave the impression that it was an intentional execution attempt. Was it planned?

He was determined to go ahead, now more than ever. For Rose... and for himself. This scum did not care about anything or anyone. They would stop at nothing to get rid of any inconveniences.

He had to be faster and outsmart them. He hoped with all his heart that Rose would recover. According to her sister the doctors were quite positive about her chances. Besides, Rose was strong.

He could not accept that these scoundrels got away with it. From the hallway next to the emergency room he dialed Beth's number.

"Beth, they've hurt Rose... She was thrown from a vehicle and was found in a critical condition in the street. The doctors are still struggling to get her out of the coma, but they think she will be okay..." he finished.

"I'm so sorry Jeff. I know you really care for her. Tell me what do you want us to do?," she said in a concerned tone that did not sound entirely convincing.

"I think we should continue... for her and for us," he said.

They discussed what their next steps would be and get right down to it immediately.

He hailed for a taxi and returned home. He had a hard time falling asleep overthinking the events of the day and the reasons behind it.

After tossing and turning for about an hour, he got up and prepared himself some hot mint tea. He took his old violin from its case and ended up in his study with his mint tea and the violin. That was the room furthest away from the neighbors in which he installed sound proofing years ago. Even so, it was very late and he placed the mute on the bridge of the violin. He began to practice the piece he longed for at that moment: Paganini's sonata number 6.

After several hours of feverish playing he collapsed into a restless sleep on the sofa and spent most of the night there tortured by nightmares.

9. The agency

He woke up feeling especially tired. It required true effort and determination to drag himself from bed. He was unsure of when and how he got to bed as the last thing he remembered was lying on the sofa in the study.

The alarm clock rang too many times to remember. He was not someone who liked staying in bed more than ten minutes after waking up. Jeff had nightmares all night and his head was pounding as if he attended a six-hour programming conference without a break.

He needed a strong coffee to wake himself up and clear his foggy mind after a night in which he barely slept for half an hour.

With great effort he dragged himself from bed and stumbled to the bathroom where he washed his face with plenty of water in the hope to gain some level of lucidity.

Standing in the kitchen of his loft waiting for the coffee machine to prepare the precious black liquid, he could not prevent the flashing images of the last twenty-eight hours from entering his mind. How he woke up from being drugged at the office, his plea for help, the kidnapping of Rose and submitting to the wishes of the extortionists. And Rose....

He knew beforehand that the coffee would make him sick because of his strange allergic reaction to almost anything.

He was willing to take that chance though. At this point he considered the effect of the caffeine more beneficial than the side effects from his intolerance. In the past when he resorted to such drastic measures it proved to outweigh the adverse effects.

Why he still had the coffee machine was unclear. At first he thought he would keep it to offer coffee to his guests, but it has been years since he last had any visitors. However, he never lost hope. He slowly sipped the last few drops of the pick me up liquid and left his flat.

In the street he stopped for a moment right in front of the entrance of his building to enjoy the fresh morning air. Although he wasn't really mad about the cold climate of the city, he had to concede that there was nothing like it to clear your mind in the morning.

He took the N-line to Manhattan and got off at his usual stop. In recent years he had repeated this exact routine so many times that he could do it blindfolded. He would often rest his head against the cold glass of the car, as many other travelers did, and allow his mind to drift.

He has gone through many creative phases inspiring him to write some short stories on his forty minute daily journeys. For that reason he always carried a small notebook in his bag. He never knew when the muse would smile upon him.

On this occasion however, he was in a state of drowsiness that prevented such a thought to even enter his mind. The whole trip he had trouble keeping awake, propping up his head against the window and trying to clear his mind. He was afraid of falling into a deep sleep and missing his stop.

Five minutes before reaching the stop at the company, he would get up to stretch his legs. That was practically the only exercise he got during his daily routine.

Once in the hall of the building where his company rented several floors, he waited patiently with coworkers for a lift to arrive on the ground floor.

Consumed by his own thoughts, he suddenly noticed someone inserting something into the outer right pocket of his jacket. A voice whispered in his ear: "Jeff, don't open it now. Wait 'till you be alone."

Wow! This was truly becoming like a police drama. Who would have guessed a few hours ago that he would get embroiled in such an absurd plot...

He turned around, but could not see the person who had left the letter. He took it out of his pocket and could see that it was a folio folded into four parts. As instructed he put it back into his pocket to read when he was alone. A few minutes would still pass for him to reach his floor before he could do that.

There is nothing as slow as a lift stopping on each floor for people to get on or off. At one point he even calculated that on average he stopped at least 8 times before reaching his floor. On this morning it felt even longer as he was burning to see what message the mysterious note contained.

He felt sure that it had something to do with events that uprooted his life during the past hours. It was unclear as to why they would now communicate with notes. So far messages were only conveyed by phone.

The real problem was that he had no privacy at his desk as he was temporarily placed in the hallway while the offices were refurbished. This "temporary" arrangement lasted for almost four years. Apart from the obvious fact of having no privacy, it also posed a security risk in his line of work.

It is not that he was the typical computer scientist who ploughed through pages of dubious content. More often than not he would give his imagination free reign to navigate freely through the network of all networks. He did however find that his workstation in the middle of the corridor cramped his style and increased his stress levels.

As on so many other occasions before, he had to visit the toilets to get some privacy. He opened the door and chose one of the stalls farthest from the entrance. Once it was bolted shut, he pulled the paper from his jacket.

His first impression was correct. A tiny grin appeared on his face. He could not help it, he loved being right. His mind was superior and his special superpower. Even as a child he experienced this reaction, both in class and when playing with the other children in the park.

At last he began to read the mysterious letter:

```
Jeff: This situation has spiralled out of
control. Stay out of it or you will live to
regret it. This is your final warning.
A.
```

He was totally taken aback by this turn of events. It was not that out of the ordinary for his previous employer, The Agency, as he liked to call it, to stick their noses into other people's business. In fact it all made perfect sense as this whole mess smacked of their involvement. They took care to make their presence felt.

On the other hand, it was quite strange that they even bothered to contact him in person to warn him. When he used to work for the agency they did not waste any time on such trivial things and simply pursued their own interests ruthlessly.

If anything or anyone crossed or annoyed them, they got rid of it. He did not really fulfill any crucial role in their dubious dealings other than assessing obtained data to certify its origin.

After such a direct threat it was important to to weigh all the pros and cons of non-compliance. As a former employee of the agency he had enough inside information to know the dangers of ignoring the letter.

It was definitely not something that could be taken lightly.

He remained seated on the toilet bowl for another ten minutes while the core of his CPU ran at full speed.

The coffee he drank at home gave him the energy and clarity of mind that would otherwise have been impossible after the terrible night he had.

Instinctively he knew the first thing to do was to let Beth know what was going on, but he decided against it as he was scared this would endanger her life. After what happened to Rose he was not prepared to take any chances. They never considered involving the police because of a lack of trust and all the red tape involved.

He was also convinced that the police was not agile enough to act at the speed this operation required. In addition there was so much money involved putting the company in a precarious position. It was definitely better not to involve too many people.

Either way, it was not his decision to make either. The director also felt it was better to keep things under wraps given the situation.

This was undoubtedly the most difficult decision he ever had to make. Both options were equally bad. His company stood to lose a vast amount of money if he remained quiet as the agency required of him. If he took matters into his own hands, people, including himself, could get hurt. On the other hand if he were to involve more people it could actually make matters worse as that could endanger their lives as well.

After a lot of consideration he decided to postpone a final decision. He came out of the toilet stall and washed his face with a generous amount of cold water. He stared at his own reflection in the mirror for a long time.

It always surprised him how much his appearance could change with a little water in his hair. He felt that the few minutes of seclusion afforded his head the clarity it was crying out for. The cold water on his face and nape also helped to clear the cobwebs from his mind.

He finally left the toilet and went to the hall where his table was. He flopped down in his chair with his elbows resting on the edge of the desk. He clutched his head with his hands, revealing his feelings of total desperation.

He lost track of time and entered a state of disconnectedness. It was as if his brain had short circuited. The terrible night and all the stress during the past few hours now really took its toll. He was now on the edge of breakpoint.

From afar he could hear a female voice calling him. Little by little the voice became clearer until he could hear her right by his side. He opened his eyes as best he could and tried to focus on the figure next to him. He was unsure who it was, but he knew it was a woman. When he regained some degree of clarity he could tell that it was Linda.

He leaned back into the chair and he stared at her. With a stern look she asked him why he was sleeping in plain sight there at his workstation in the corridor. He looked at his wristwatch and understood perfectly what she meant. More than ninety minutes had passed since he left the toilet. He again lost consciousness at his desk. This time for more than an hour and a half and of course he did not remember anything at all.

He awkwardly apologised to her for falling asleep at his table. After explaining that he had a very bad night with hardly any sleep, he told her that he was going to ask permission to go home and rest.

She accepted his explanation and in turn apologised for being so hard on him. Actually Linda had no jurisdiction over him to reprimand him like that, but it would be very bad indeed if she reported him to Daniel.

Although she overreacted, Linda was quite right that he should not be caught sleeping on duty. His exhaustion was caused by work related matters but the less suspicion he raised the better.

He took the opportunity to ask her about the mysterious visitor hanging around his desk the other day. She remembered him well and told him everything she could, but it was not much.

He couldn't really remember the first time he saw her. She joined the company much later than he did. If his memory didn't fail him it must have been four or five years after his joint to the company. It was curious how some people seemed to climb the corporate ladder so much faster than others. He couldn't help but wonder if she had to do some favours on her way up.

She entered the company nothing more than a bellhop and within a few months she was in charge of reception. By the end of the following year she moved to the Security Department. She was pretty though. They did not have many opportunities to socialise so he did not really know much about her. He did not even know whether she had a family or not. That often happened in bigger companies.

10. Faith that moves mountains

Thus far all ways they have pursued ended up in a deadlock. He was at a total loss as to what the next step should be. He already dragged Rose and Beth into the equation but everything spiralled out of control with no sign of any progress. At least he knew that Beth was trying to buy them time to counter the theft and, of course, to avenge Rose.

He had an uneasy feeling that a vital piece was missing from the puzzle. He could not understand how the infiltrator managed to find out that EADAR was their client and moreover that they had vast sums of money that could be syphoned off in the way they were doing it.

He made his way to Daniel's office and hesitated at the door contemplating whether he was doing the right thing. He didn't know how to approach the matter. "Hello Daniel, they are stealing a client's money right under our noses, and besides, they are using our servers to do it." It was very… tricky at best.

At last he knocked on the door and waited for the invitation to enter. After a few seconds, he opened the door and saw Daniel sitting at his desk. A man dressed in a black trench coat was in deep conversation with him. Daniel seemed upset with the worry clearly visible on his face.

Noticing Jeff at the door, Daniel glared at him and with his eyes gave a signal to disappear immediately, which he did. He took a seat on one of the chairs in the hallway and waited for the meeting with the stranger to end.

Something about Daniel's visitor was bloodcurdling familiar despite his hat, scarf and sunglasses. The outfit was obviously chosen to conceal his identity, but Jeff's analytical mind did however recognize the man behind the disguise.

He immediately went into Daniel's office after the stranger left and found him with his head in his hands in total desperation. He didn't even look up but invited Jeff to sit with a shaky voice.

"What happened, what did you do, Daniel?" he asked.

"Hold on, give me a minute to calm down," he said in a pitiful voice.

Suddenly everything started to make sense to Jeff. Daniel was the one who got the client and he was surely instrumental in the software breach that gave rise to the millions being embezzled.

"I'm so sorry, Jeff. They discovered my weakness and threatened me into cooperating with them. It has been a few months now that I have been providing them with inside information on everything we were doing for EADAR."

"Why are you telling me all this now, Daniel?"

Daniel dropped his head into his hands again, rubbing his scalp rhythmically, as if the massage would help him concentrate.

"I'm dead, Jeff"

"What?"

"After what they did to Rose, I refused to collaborate anymore. They have come to give me an ultimatum, which I have not accepted. Will you tell her that I am very sorry and that I love her?"

Jeff's head was spinning. Suddenly nothing made sense anymore. Daniel looked sincere as if he was telling the truth, but he didn't understand how all the pieces fit together.

"I don't understand, Daniel. Tell what... to whom?"

"I don't know how to start Jeff. It all happened unintentionally.

You were no longer with her. We went out a couple of times and discovered that we were made for each other."

"Damn, that was it," said to himself.

"We didn't want to cause you any pain. We thought that after a few months you would be over the breakup and it would be easier to tell you the truth. But you didn't stop hovering by her side. We both realised that it was a bad time for you and tried to keep it under wraps," he continued. "What I don't know is how they found out about us," he said in a sob.

"This at least concludes the mole chapter," Jeff murmured grudgingly.

Now that everything was out in the open, he intended to get every last detail from Daniel. And above all, why he thought that he had a death sentence. No matter how badly they behaved, he did not deserve to die. Besides, it appeared that he was in this mess precisely because he tried to protect Rose. Or so it seemed at this point at least.

While his supervisor was on a guilt trip his thoughts wandered to the afternoon Rose broke up with him. They used to leave work together going to her house and then later he would either take the long walk or the subway to his flat.

He could not recall exactly how the argument started. They had several arguments the previous week, but on that day it was especially bad. She was convinced that he was having an affair behind her back with someone at the office. It was true that in New York affairs were not really a big deal, but she made it very clear that she would not tolerate it as long as they were together.

Now, in hindsight, he could clearly see how she played him with the necessary drama. He looked back at the events as if he had a seat in the front row watching her Oscar-worthy performance as best actress.

A broken voice brought him back to reality...

"Now that Rose is like this and I have received a death threat, I want to tell you everything you need to know to put an end to this," he managed to finish.

"Well, let's do that then," Jeff said. " I can hardly believe what you're telling me about you and Rose. Firstly, I've been mislead all this time, thinking I had a chance of getting back with her again... ," he paused as if waiting for an answer, "... and secondly: What is this story about your life being in danger? I don't think you should be so melodramatic... ," he waited for Daniel to say something this time.

A few seconds passed, and Daniel, swallowing hard, remained silent.

"I've been asked to do something... something I can't do... I've refused. With Rose in her current condition and when the truth of what really happened comes out, I would rather be dead... ," he paused for a breath, "and I have already told them that I won't do what I have been instructed. I told them that the buck stops here, I am getting out."

"I don't think you should stop now, after what you've already done. Rather try to buy some time. What exactly did they ask you to do?"

"It's simple... they want me... to kill you. Tonight. If I don't, they'll send one of their henchmen to get rid of me," he took another breath, "I refuse to kill or have a death on my conscience, and much less yours. I'd rather die myself"

The rest of the meeting focused on other shared interests and talking about both Rose and the case.

When Jeff got the full picture of everything that had happened, at least from Daniel's point of view, he tried to reassure him:

"The big boss knows everything. Don't do anything crazy. Stay here and wait for me to come back. I'll brief him about the situation and I'm sure he will be able to think about a solution."

With that he left the office, closing the door carefully behind him.

On his way to the floor of his superior, he was totally absorbed in his thoughts about what was happening. Daniel's statements definitely cast a whole new light on the subject. He was so deeply in thought that he walked the whole way automatically. If he met or spoke to someone on the way he would certainly not remember it.

When he reached the chief's office, he was not there. He looked at his watch and knew the reason all too well. Normally the big bosses would finish their working day at noon They were however available on their cell phones 24 hours a day.

For a moment he considered whether this might the right time to make that call and disturb him. He decided against it. He left Daniel alone and on second thoughts did not think it was a good idea to do so. He turned around and walked back as fast as he could. This time his thoughts were focused on his supervisor. He did not want anything to happen to him.

When he returned to Daniel's office, he found the door slightly ajar and the office dark. The light from the hallway seeped through the slit, revealing a dantesque scene. As he opened the door, light from the hallway flooded in to reveal the spectacle inside. At that moment he really regretted not staying with Daniel or at least taking him along with him...

He reached for the light switch but the click it made when he switched it on did not seem normal. His instincts kicked in and he reacted quickly. He managed to see legs sticking out from behind the table just before the explosion.

The noise was deafening. He felt somewhat dizzy from the noise and deflagration. He tried to crawl into the office, but the fire had begun to devour the table and was already licking up the shelves. He was not an expert on explosives but he knew that this was done by a professional.

The fire alarm went off by itself and in a few seconds the hallway was flooded by staff trying to evacuate the floor. He tried to get one of them to stop and help him drag, what he believed to be Daniel's lifeless body, from the office.

The flames spread like wildfire and the floor would soon be

impenetrable. After a few seconds of intense contemplation, he decided to join the fleeing staff. He again deeply regretted not staying with Daniel. Involuntary memories of the day he did his interview for a position at the company came to mind.

"Sit down please. My name is Daniel Roberts and I will be evaluating you for the web developer position."

"Pleased to meet you. My name is ..."

"Jeff Patterson, I know, no need to waste time. I am looking for a highly competent person with clear ideas. If you are that person, the position is yours."

He remembered it as if it were yesterday, totally oblivious of the terrified cries of his colleagues around him who ran like sheep looking for an emergency exit.

"But no tests. So, nothing else?" Jeff asked

"I've seen your resume and I firmly believe that you are the person we need. Besides, if there is a problem, the company will not think twice before saying goodbye. It is much easier to leave than to enter. Although, as you see, entering is not that difficult either."

"I agree and I accept!"

He woke up lying on his back in an ambulance with an oxygen mask on his face. The health worker explained that he lost consciousness because of smoke inhalation and that he was very lucky that a coworker carried him down to the ground floor.

He was lying on the stretcher for a long time. A nurse checked on him several times.

"How do you feel?" she asked.

"A little disoriented" Jeff stammered.

"It's quite normal, don't worry about it. I'll give you ten more minutes. If you don't feel strong enough to go home, I will admit you to hospital for observation." She turned to take care of other patients.

He could not waste any more time. That was a luxury he could not afford right now. He took longer and deeper breaths in an attempt to oxygenate his brain and regain complete consciousness.

He looked at his wrist watch to see how much time he had until the nurse came again. He stretched his arms within the confines of the ambulance and within a few minutes he tried to sit up. He took a few more minutes but was unable to muster the necessary strength.

Eventually, just as the nurse returned, he managed to sit up normally. He removed the oxygen mask from his face and took several deep breaths. He was feeling fairly lucid and asked for help to get to his feet. As he was not dizzy anymore, he asked to be discharged.

A taxi drove him home. When he reached the landing at his door, a surprise was awaiting him. The lock had been forced and papers were strewn all over the flat. Surely they were not looking for anything. It looked more like a statement to show him how inconsequential he was and subject to their whim.

He cleared the things from the couch and sat down with his head in his hands trying to compose himself.

11. No return

The situation really got out of hand, Jeff thought to himself. With the Agency hot on my tracks, Daniel dead, Rose critically injured and who knows what might happen next.

Almost fifty hours had passed since the whole mess began. So far everything that could go wrong, did. It was time to consider all options carefully and make a sensible decision.

His pride egged him on to unravel the whole plot, unmask who was behind it and clear his name. However, he knew full well that the machinery he was up against was well oiled to get away with it. It did not really matter that he had been a part of that very same machinery for some time and knew quite well how it worked. He felt tired and somewhat overwhelmed.

The whole matter of Rose was also weighing heavily on his mind. During the past few days his feelings for her were revived. Feelings he thought he overcame. Now that she was out of the coma, he considered declaring his love for her, hoping she would reciprocate. He was unsure whether it was her condition and the fear of losing her that urged him to do something he was not hundred percent sure of.

On the other hand, being with Beth also brought back some tender memories. He was really messed up. They became inseparable, forced together by circumstances and the Agency being hot on their trail all the time. All of that gave rise to these conflicting feelings.

He dropped onto the couch with his head in his hands. He needed to take a break to think clearly about everything. The red lights flashing in his mind pointed directly at the exit, signaling the only escape from all this.

Meanwhile, in another part of the world...

A striking brunette of medium stature stood at a large window, her big brown eyes staring into the distance. She wore a pencil skirt, light blouse and black court shoes that gave her an appearance far too serious for such a beautiful young woman. The starkness of her gaze and a firmness around her mouth were telling signs that life had not been easy for her.

A uniformed man entered the room behind her and brought her back from her thoughts as he clicked his heels together in salute to his superior. She turned around and listened somewhat distracted as his superior asked him:

"Progress report on the EADAR operation, Sergeant."

"Everything is running according to plan. We have slowed the transfer of funds somewhat as to not raise too many suspicions. We are now at 0.8 per day. At this rate we shall reach our final goal in less than a month, Captain."

The officer turned to the beautiful woman and said,

"As promised, Olivia."

She nodded slightly and turned to rest her body against the window sill. She looked away and let her mind wander.

Finally she was going to get justice for the death of her father at the hands of EADAR's hired assassins all those years ago. The case was never solved and the charges were dropped for a lack of evidence. The strange circumstances of his death made it impossible to pinpoint the culprit. But she knew the truth. The words of her father that night still echoed clearly in her head.

She managed to review his documentation years later, after bribing some former employees of EADAR. Luckily the young detective on the case, Alex, also gave his help when she started her own investigation.

More than once she imagined herself with Alex. The age difference was a pity though and on top of that she was still suffering from the intense trauma caused by the horrible death of her father. Her terrible past stood in the way of any kind of meaningful relationship.

Now, after so many years, she brought together a whole team of professionals to wage her own private vendetta against EADAR, but somehow the fact that everything was falling into place now felt empty and without any ring of victory. Nothing could bring back her father. The knowledge that she could bring them to their knees due to a lack of funds created a warped sense of satisfaction.

She sometimes found it very difficult to make harsh decisions to keep the ball rolling. Her only condition was to never harm innocent people outside the management of the company. It was thus a matter of great anguish to her learning that a civilian by the name Rose got seriously injured and could have died in the course of her plan. Although they planned the whole operation meticulously, they never counted on the persistent intrusion of Jeff Patterson. His resourcefulness constantly put a spanner in the works.

Many years ago she might have fallen in love with a guy like that, but her burning desire for revenge distracted her from any normal relationships. Maybe now that everything was coming to a head, she might regain some sense of normality in her own life.

At this point however she wished that Jeff would just disappear from the face of the earth and allow her to finally drain EADAR of every last cent.

She was still undecided as to what to do with all the money. Of course she had to pay the Captain and his team their dues, but she was not sure of what to do with the rest.

It was most likely that she would donate the money to some NGO to alleviate her guilt a little. As for Daniel's death, she never agreed for that to happen at any point in time. The Captain however insisted that he had not been killed. They might have overreached the scope of their influence slightly.

She leaned her head against the cold glass and a tear rolled down her cheek.

"I love you, Dad," said in a whisper.

Back in Manhattan

Beth was deeply worried about the events of the last few hours. Rose was seriously injured, Jeff beside himself with worry and she… she found herself rekindling her long lost love for Jeff. She thought she was over him, but that appeared to not be the case at all.

It was said that you never forget your first love. Although Jeff was not technically her first, he was actually her first true love.

She didn't know what to do next. For the first time since she graduated she felt lost and without any concrete plan of how to proceed. One thing was certain though: something had to be done. There were so many people involved and so much was at stake that they urgently needed to decide on a course of action.

She stood pensively in front of her desk and finally opened one of the drawers. For a moment she stared at a large envelope under a few bundles of keys. She took out the envelope and emptied its contents on the table: her passport, a thousand dollars in cash and a couple of credit cards.

Since she started in this odd profession she always knew that this day would come. It did not arrive the way she expected or planned though. Rather than having to flee for something she had done, she was going on the run for something that happened to Jeff. She was in all this well over her head. Because of her involvement she would certainly not go unpunished.

She stared mesmerized at the items on the desk like a Shaman at the bones from where he expected some guidance for the future. She shook her head, grabbed the items and stuffed them into her backpack. Hurriedly she dialed a number from her cell phone and waited for it to be answered...

"Jeff, we have to disappear. I've got my passport and some money. I'll pick you up in twenty minutes," she said in a decisive voice.

After a pause of a few seconds on the line:

"... okay, I agree. But there is something I have to do before we go. We can do it on our way. I'll wait for you at the entrance of my building," he said.

Jeff filled a small suitcase with what he considered to be the most essential things. He was not fleeing a natural disaster like an earthquake, but it almost felt like it. It felt as if his life and whole existence was hanging by a thread. This was not the time for bouts of melancholy or anxiety about the past or future. Nor was it a time to worry about trivialities. He needed to focus on basic items of clothing and toiletries. The rest could be purchased wherever they were going. Besides being a piece of junk, his laptop could cause problems as it might give away their whereabouts. It was far better to rather use public computers if and when needed.

He still had two minutes left and waited patiently inside the building. He didn't want to risk unnecessary exposure that might draw unwanted attention to their plans.

He went to see Rose one last time. At least that's what Jeff told Beth on their way to the hospital.

"I just want to make sure she's all right," he told her.

They climbed the steps to the building together as nothing in the world could convince Beth to wait alone in the car. From that day their lives would be intertwined forever. In some way fleeing together somehow sentenced them to being together.

Only Jeff entered Rose's room as the ICU had strict rules allowing only one visitor at a time.

In the waiting room Beth was pacing up and down biting her nails. She thought that she kicked this bad habit years ago, but the tension made her so nervous that she started again. She instinctively knew Jeff did not tell her the whole truth. From the way he spoke about Rose she could pick up that he still had feelings for her. A woman notices these things.

She looked through the glass partition of the intensive care room and saw Jeff taking Rose's hand...

"Rose, I've been thinking... I've had a very hard time these past few days. I thought you were dying. The doctors say you are concussed and suffering from temporary amnesia but that you will recover. I want us to be together again... if you also want that," he paused to catch his breath.

She bravely tried to speak and then signalled with her eyes for him to come closer. Jeff bent over her with his ear close to her mouth.

"Jeff, I did love you, but not anymore. What happened between us was very special and I will never forget it. Try to make a fresh start without me," she said in a faint voice.

Beth observed the intimate scene, blushed slightly and turned away to afford them some privacy. She couldn't hear what they were saying, but it looked as if they were either making peace or declaring their love for each other. Finally she gave up trying to figure out what was happening and headed for the row of chairs in the waiting room.

Although Jeff spent little more than five minutes with Rose, it felt like an eternity. During this time all her plans for the future started to evaporate before her eyes. Was she only jealous or a bit crazy?

Once in the car Jeff began to speak before they even left the parking lot.

"We finally broke up... I believed what we had could be salvaged and revived, but that was not the case. The feeling wasn't mutual."

She smiled faintly, turned slowly towards him and gave him a long kiss.

"I love you," she said softly.

Together they drove off.

12. Closing the circle

Before leaving the big apple they made several stops at ATMs, withdrawing everything they could. When the credit limits of both their accounts were reached, they decided to get rid of the cards. The best way to go unnoticed is by paying cash and avoiding crowded areas with security cameras. Beth knew everything about going off the radar. For many years it was her job to keep track of people following their electronic payment trails.

They wanted their trail to end in New York and not make use of the electronic payment system when they crossed some of the bridges. They managed to raise a healthy sum of money but it was certainly not enough to start a new life.

Beth told Jeff that she had some friends in Boston who would take them in for a few days. Good people, she said. They did not have many options available to them and it was absolutely imperative to keep moving. Going north, they avoided the main roads as far as possible. In a couple of days they would be in Boston.

A road trip that would normally take no more than 8 hours, took them more than double the amount of time. They avoided the interstates taking turns sleeping and driving. They did not want to make more stops than were absolutely necessary. The county highways were less than ideal to run, but they provided the much needed cover and safety.

Sleeping in the car and taking turns to drive also minimized the cost which, from now on, they had to be very careful about. The stops consisted mainly of filling up the car, buying refreshments and the essential bathroom visits.

When they reached the outskirts of Boston they looked for cell phone shop. They destroyed and disposed of their cell phones in New York. To contact Beth's friends they needed to get a disposable phone.

Thanks to Beth's unfailing memory, they were able contact her friends, who after the initial surprise, were glad to welcome them at their home. They drove with a determined air to the address provided and in a little less of than an hour they were there.

It was a small three-story cottage in the Harvard area, where dozens of students swarmed along pedestrian paths between the schools. On the sidewalk, just outside the number they had been given over the phone, a familiar face awaited them.

Beth's friend who was waiting for them at the gate looked nice but sober at the same time. A full beard and disproportionate spectacles gave him the true geek appearance. The blond hair and his chiseled features suggested a northern European origin, probably Scandinavian. Jeff could even imagine him wearing a Viking helmet, but on the other hand, the finest specimen of the human race.

It was not a problem to find a parking spot, and they left the vehicle within yards of Beth's friend.

After the appropriate introductions on the sidewalk, they went upstairs. A pleasant woman received them with hugs and kisses. Beth's friends explained that the upper floor was rented out to students and that they had a free room, which they could use for as long as they wanted.

They left their things on the bed in their room and went out onto the porch with their new friends. The warmth and friendliness with which the couple received them put Jeff in a very good mood allowing him to forget the mess they were in for a few hours. They chatted about news events and the past but at no point did the couple probe the reasons for them being there. He agreed beforehand with Beth to only share information on a need to know base as too much information might put their lives at risk. The first night they spent together felt a little odd. The room only had one big double bed, but neither of them had any objections to sharing a bed. In truth the events of the last few days united them like never before. The contact of her feet during the night evoked fond memories and aroused Jeff.

"Do you want to make love?" he said in a whisper.

She half opened her eyes and lazily looked at him in the street light filtering through the blinds and trees outside. It created moving patterns of dusk in the room.

During his dating years Jeff discovered that the normal pickup lines did not work. At least not for the kind of girls he cared about. They liked a direct but softer approach. It did not really increase his chances of success, but it did have more positive responses from the girls he found attractive. The situation now was a bit uncomfortable. Two adults in the same bed.

Two adults who already knew each other well and had relations in the past. Being direct could not be misunderstood.

"What makes you think I want to?" she said, also whispering.

He promptly shut her mouth with a moist and tender kiss. Not too sexual, at least not at first. She responded to his caresses and Jeff started to undress her enjoying the pleasant feeling of being naked with her under the sheets. The fact that they were fleeing together served to make their bond even stronger.

Beth knew for sure that Jeff had not completely forgotten Rose. But she also knew he was with her now. Things had turned out this way and there was no turning back.

They slept spooning and naked the rest of the night.

They woke up smiling for much of the morning, sharing

affectionate giggles when the looked at each other.

For a few days they felt as if they did not have a care in the world. They enjoyed every moment of each other's company and their new found friends.

In the days following that they drew up a plan. They knew for sure that disappearing from New York would not at all deter those who followed them. Jeff told Beth several times that they did not appear to be people who liked to leave dead ends.

They prioritised the various actions to be carried out to get clarity of where to start. Neither of them ever had to flee for their lives so agreed to be very open minded and analytical about their options.

One of the first things they did was to get rid of the car. With a home base to return to it seemed logical to dump the car.. They decided to take a trip to Springfield and leave it parked on a street.

Besides it being a day that would allow them to enjoy each other's company, it would also increase their chances of escape.

Once there, they bought bus tickets for Boston and abandoned the car. It was well parked on a quiet street. They checked that there were no signs restricting parking or anything that would cause the car to be towed away. They did not want the licence plate and its owner published over there to remove the car. The longer the vehicle could go undetected the better. Time was very precious to them.

The bus ride was uneventful and they enjoyed the warmth of holding each other's hands while the countryside passed by the big windows of the vehicle.

Back in Boston they talked to Beth's friends and told them, without too many details that could be incriminating, the reason for their visit. In the end they decided that they deserved even to at least know part of the truth.

Their friends were totally mesmerized by their story and looked at them with incredulity and admiration. Suddenly they were celebrity superheroes in their friend's eyes. It was a miracle how they managed to keep up their daily jobs to put food on the table and at the same time outwit intrepid assassins hot on their trail.

After the initial shock and disbelief both started to plan the best course of action for Jeff and Beth. The fact that they drove to Boston in their own car was not a good idea and even though they got rid of it, the damage might have been done already.

Several alternatives were put on the table for discussion but in the end the least obvious option seemed to convince the couple.

Beth's friends had an acquaintance in government. A Senator's assistant, although they were not quite sure. Most of the time this person resided in Washington DC.

The plan seemed simple enough. They would go to Washington DC and talk to the person in government in an effort to obtain some kind of immunity. If they failed or did not manage to see him, they were destined to be on the run for the rest of their lives.

After several days of preparations and planning for all eventualities they might encounter, they decided to take a leap of faith. After a brief farewell they left for the bus station.

The journey was monotonous and boring. Both were caught up in their own thoughts about the predicament they were in. Beth, who only recently realised the true magnitude of their problem, fervently wished she never agreed to help Jeff when he called her. Jeff on the other hand recurrently thought he should have put the matter in the hands of the police from the beginning.

With their hands entwined and worried faces both of them looked straight ahead without really seeing anything. They did not dare discuss it for fear of laying bare their true feelings about the matter. Despite their sombre thoughts and rattling of the bus, both of them fell into the arms of Morpheus with their heads against each others.

The uncomfortable sleep did refresh them to a certain extent and they arrived in Washington DC with new energy to tackle their problem. They decided to rent a locker to store all they had of value. A place to stay for a few days was their next priority. Although money was not a problem at the time, they had to be frugal because they did not know how long they might have to survive on it. They decided not to spend too much on accommodation and that a shared room in a simpler neighbourhood would be more than enough.

Very early the next day they received a call on the disposable phone. It was one of their friends from Boston who had difficulty expressing himself due to his emotional state. He told them that they were visited by men from some government department and threatened with imprisonment if they did not cooperate. To win some time they told them that they sheltered them for a few days and that they were on their way to Springfield.

It seemed as if fate was playing a macabre trick on them. They could not rest on their laurels and needed to find the assistant of the Senator immediately or leave that city as their lives depended on it.

After several efforts at the Capitol, they realised it was impossible to locate the assistant at the moment. He apparently took a little vacation at the same time as his boss. Deflated and without much hope they made their way to the bus station.

At the bus station they discovered that the locker where they deposited all they had, including the money, had been forced leaving them with nothing except the clothes on their backs.

Beth could not contain her tears and hugged Jeff sobbing uncontrollably. Tears ran over Jeff's cheeks as well as they hugged each other for a long time.

They stood there for a long time hugging, trying to comfort each other. She eventually loosened her grip, looked into his eyes and asked:

"What are we going to do, Jeff?"

He hesitated a moment and then wiped the tears from her eyes with the back of his hands. All he could manage to say was: "I don't know honey."